MR 14 '03

THE BEAST ARISES

The Beast Arises

26

LEFT BEHIND

>THE KIDS<

Jerry B. Jenkins

Tim LaHaye

WITH CHRIS FABRY

TYNDALE HOUSE PUBLISHERS, INC.
WHEATON, ILLINOIS

Visit Tyndale's exciting Web site at www.tyndale.com

Discover the latest Left Behind news at www.leftbehind.com

Published in association with the literary agency of Alive Communications, Inc., 7680 Goddard Street, Suite 200, Colorado Springs, CO 80920.

Edited by Curtis H. C. Lundgren

ISBN 0-8423-5790-4, mass paper

Printed in the United States of America

08 07 06 05 04 03
9   8   7   6   5   4   3   2   1

To Josh, Abby, Dina, and Curt

Table of Contents

What's Gone On Before

JUDD Thompson Jr. and the rest of the Young Tribulation Force are living the adventure of a lifetime. In Israel, Judd stops his friend Kasim from assassinating Nicolae Carpathia, but Kasim runs away. Later, Nicolae executes the two witnesses, Eli and Moishe, in front of an elated crowd at the Wailing Wall.

Vicki Byrne and her friends in Illinois narrowly escape Global Community Peacekeepers and Morale Monitors. The kids abandon the schoolhouse and meet a farmer and his wife. Charlie decides to stay with the couple. Vicki and the others drive to Wisconsin to the summer home of Darrion Stahley. While the kids watch the incredible events in Israel, Darrion tells Vicki about a disturbing memory.

While Judd spots Kasim at the Wailing Wall and races after him, Lionel Washington watches the dead bodies of Eli and Moishe come back to life. After the two rise to heaven in a cloud, a devastating earthquake rocks Jerusalem. As buildings crash in the distance, Lionel rushes into the death zone, wondering if Judd is still alive.

Join the Young Tribulation Force as they watch a deadly prophecy unfold before their eyes.

ONE

Judd's Discovery

JUDD ran after Kasim, losing sight of him in the crowd. He hated leaving the Wailing Wall, but he couldn't let Kasim get away again. Judd had to convince him to abandon his assassination plot.

The streets were filled with vendors and drunken people still celebrating the witnesses' deaths. He elbowed his way through a crowd watching a television and jumped to see over the crowd. Kasim turned a corner and ran away.

A man pointed at the television and laughed. "Look at that. Three days and they're still dead."

The screaming vocals of Z-Van and The Four Horsemen drowned the crowd's laughter. Judd rounded the corner as Kasim disappeared into a group on the side of the street. A banner over a music store ahead read

1

"Meet Z-Van today!" For a hundred Nicks, fans could receive a signed copy of The Four Horsemen's latest recording.

A woman screamed and ran from a bar, both hands over her mouth. She knelt on the sidewalk. A middle-aged man followed her outside, pale and shaking. "They're alive!"

Judd ran to the bar as people streamed out, toppling chairs and tables. Judd pushed his way to the window and saw Eli and Moishe—alive! The two witnesses struggled to their feet, their chests heaving, their faces turned toward the sky.

Judd clenched his fists. "Yes!"

The street was alive now, people rushing back and forth, not believing the news. People near the music store darted out of line and rushed toward alleys. Others seemed confused. A window smashed and several people reached through and grabbed recordings. A rumor spread through the throng that Eli and Moishe were on their way to the main stage.

"That means they'll come straight through here!" someone said.

A few laughed, not believing the reports. "Those two have been dead three days," a man yelled. "They're not going anywhere."

A voice so loud Judd thought it had come from the speakers a few feet away said, "COME UP HERE!" The sun peeked through snow-white clouds, and the rays cast beautiful colors over the crowd.

"Look there!" a woman screeched.

Just above the buildings, Eli and Moishe rose like human hot-air balloons. People gasped and fell to their knees. The man who had laughed at the witnesses grabbed his chest and fell backward, knocking others to the ground.

Eli and Moishe were soon enveloped in white, the cloud picking up speed until it became a speck in the sky. Judd breathed a prayer of thanks.

When he opened his eyes, only a few people stood. Most lay flat, crying, moaning, begging God not to kill them. One person moved over the prostrate bodies toward the music store. It was Kasim.

Judd called to him, but as Kasim ducked inside the store, the street shattered. People flew in the air like missiles and crashed through windows. A woman was tossed into a tree and grabbed a branch. She held on a few seconds, then plunged to the ground.

"Earthquake!" people shouted as the street opened in front of them. Vendors' carts tipped, spilling contents into the great cracks. Several hundred people plunged into the chasm, screaming as they fell.

Judd crawled toward a hydrant, but another shock wave knocked it over and water shot into the air. Judd scrambled for something to hold on to as freezing raindrops smashed onto his head. He threw up his hands to shield his face as the sky turned black. A car sped toward him, careening out of control. It hit a gash in the earth, flipped upside down, and skidded on its top until it dropped into the newly opened hole.

Glass and metal exploded as nearby buildings collapsed. Judd watched a tall building teeter and fall. People tried to get out of the way, but they were crushed.

The violent shaking ended, and Judd marveled at how quickly things had been destroyed. Trees lay in the street. Buildings leaned or were flattened. Judd remembered how long the wrath of the Lamb earthquake had lasted and was glad this one had lasted only a few seconds.

The dark sky gave way to sunshine again, which cast an eerie, green light on the horror around him. As he carefully walked toward the building Kasim had entered, Judd heard a weak voice behind him. "Please help me."

People hurried past, pushing Judd to the ground. When he stood, he noticed someone's hand at the edge of the crevasse. He walked a few steps, then fell to his knees and crawled. To his shock, the hand wasn't attached.

"Over here," a woman said.

A few feet away, teetering on the edge of the crater, a car lay upside down. A woman hung out of the door, her leg wedged between the seat and the car's frame.

"Don't move!" Judd said. He scooted along, careful not to jostle the earth nearby. Steam rose from the engine, and liquid dripped near the woman's head.

"Is it going to catch fire?" the woman said.

"Don't talk. Stay still."

Other than the hissing of the steam and a few people moaning and crying, the entire area had been quieted by the massive quake. There was no more celebrating or dancing. Those who could walk hurried away.

Judd looked for a chain or some rope but couldn't find any. Bits of rock and asphalt trickled into the chasm, and he knew he had to work quickly. "Raise your hands and I'll grab you!"

The woman gingerly put up an arm, and Judd reached for her hand. When she lifted the other, Judd turned away. Her left hand was gone.

The car shifted in the crumbling earth, and Judd struggled to maintain his footing.

"I don't want to die!" the woman said.

Judd slipped and fell back, and the car tipped forward. For a moment he thought it would settle, but the door creaked and closed as the car plunged into the hole, silencing the woman's screams.

Judd rolled onto his back and put his hands over his face. How much death and suffering could the world take? Shouts from nearby brought him back to reality. He stood and rushed inside the music store to look for Kasim.

Lionel fought back tears as he ran. He had just seen Eli and Moishe rise from the dead. Their bodies had been shattered by Nicolae Carpathia and had decomposed since they were murdered, but now they were whole again. The once happy crowd was terrified.

After the witnesses had risen into a cloud, the earth shook so violently that Lionel struggled to stay on his feet. A few blocks away buildings crashed, and Lionel heard the sickening crunch of metal and glass.

People who had danced around Moishe and Eli now fled the scene in panic. A light post fell on a woman and crushed her.

Mr. Stein quickly gathered the believers. "Many will die today. We must help those who are trapped." They split into four groups and rushed toward the area that had been most severely hit.

Sam Goldberg ran next to Lionel. "Do you think anyone saw Eli and Moishe on television?"

"Wouldn't doubt it," Lionel said. "It's the biggest story of the Gala, but I'll bet Carpathia cans the replay."

"Do you think they'll still have the closing ceremony tonight?"

"Carpathia doesn't let a little death and destruction stop his party."

As Lionel and the others neared the death zone, they met hundreds of dazed and wounded people. Some helped friends and family members, but most walked by themselves, crying.

Huge cracks split the street, and many cars had fallen inside. Someone screamed, and Lionel and Sam walked into an apartment building. A woman pounded on an elevator, yelling for her husband. "He went for our camera, and I heard a crash!" The woman broke down, and Sam tried to comfort her.

Lionel punched the elevator button, but the power was off. He found a sharp tool and pried open the doors. The shaft was filled with dust. He found a flashlight in a first-floor office and looked down the shaft. Snapped cables lay on top of the mangled elevator car.

"Anybody hear me down there?" Lionel shouted. His voice echoed, but no one responded.

Lionel waited a few moments for the dust to clear, then climbed down a ladder built into the shaft. He held the flashlight under his arm as he pried open the top of the elevator. He pointed the flashlight into the hole and gasped. Three people lay dead, their bodies twisted in horrible positions. One man clutched a bloodstained camera.

"Do you see him?" the woman shouted.

Lionel climbed back up. "I'm sorry, ma'am. You don't want to—"

The woman grabbed the flashlight and pushed Lionel away. Lionel and Sam went outside as the woman screamed for her husband.

In the distance a Global Community public-address truck drove through the streets. "Attention, citizens! Volunteers are needed immediately to help with relief efforts. Closing ceremonies will take place tonight as planned. Religious fanatics have stolen the bodies of the preachers. Do not fall for fairy tales of their disappearing.

Repeat: Closing ceremonies will take place tonight as planned."

Lionel and Sam looked at each other and shook their heads. They walked farther toward the earthquake zone, wondering what they would find in the rubble.

Vicki and the others at the Wisconsin hideout were fascinated by the live shot of Eli and Moishe rising into the cloud. As announcers at the scene searched for words, cameras shook and fell over. Mark rushed to the computer and composed a message to kids around the world.

> *Don't be surprised. God predicted it would happen. The Bible also predicts that a tenth of those living in Jerusalem will die because of this quake. The Global Community will probably make up something to explain Eli and Moishe rising from the dead, but there is no doubt that God is greater than a thousand Carpathias. Keep watching. There may be more surprises tonight.*

As Vicki watched the news out of Jerusalem, she wondered about Judd, Lionel, and the others. After the live shot of Eli and

Moishe, the GC said nothing about their resurrection.

"Will any believers die in this quake?" Shelly said.

"I'm not sure," Vicki said. "I think these judgments are mainly to get the attention of unbelievers, but Loretta and Donny Moore and Ryan and a bunch of other believers died in the wrath of the Lamb earthquake."

Vicki noticed Darrion sitting alone. "You were talking about how you brought some friends up here, and you're still feeling guilty about it. You want to talk some more?"

Darrion shook her head. "Wait till this is over. I need time to think."

Vicki put an arm around Darrion and looked at the television. Sirens blared and emergency crews struggled to get into the ravaged area. Vicki leaned forward as someone who looked like Judd ran past a reporter. She closed her eyes and prayed.

Judd forced his way inside the nearly collapsed doorway and put a handkerchief over his mouth and nose. It took a few moments to see through the dust. Bodies lay trapped beneath tons of rubble, and Judd wondered if he should leave.

Judd yelled Kasim's name, and someone called from the back of the building. He climbed over cash registers, stacks of music recordings, chairs, and speakers that had been set up for the special event. Most people had gotten out of the building, but he saw a few who hadn't. Some had been crushed by falling glass, others under cement. "Hang on, I'm coming!"

Sirens wailed in the distance as Judd moved debris and found a hallway that led to the back. The collapsed ceiling stopped him.

"Back here," someone yelled.

"Stay where you are. I've got to find another way." Judd forced open a rest-room door and climbed onto the sink. The ceiling hadn't fallen here, so he lifted tiles and found enough space to crawl through. But what if the building shifted?

"Help!"

Judd pulled himself up and inched through the narrow passage, pushing with his feet and crawling arm over arm. Something rumbled, and Judd put his hands over his head, thinking it was an aftershock. The ceiling held, and Judd kept crawling until he made it through.

He found himself on the other side of the collapse in what looked like a small lunchroom. A refrigerator lay on its side, the door open and food scattered on the floor. A microwave lay next to it, along with silver-ware and broken dishes.

The back door had been smashed by a concrete block. Someone was trapped underneath. Judd found the person's arm and felt for a pulse. Nothing. He crawled to the other side and saw Kasim, facedown, dead.

Judd sat back and shook his head. First Nada had been killed, now Kasim. He stood to leave when something moved behind him and a man said, "Are you going to help me or not?"

Judd went inside and saw a foot sticking out from under a smashed table. He cleared chairs away and found a man wearing a leather jacket and designer jeans pinned beneath it. Sunglasses lay a few feet away, unbroken.

"Better get me out before the whole thing comes down," the man said.

"Wait. I know you."

"Yeah, yeah, I'm Z-Van. But I'll be just another dead singer if I don't get out of here. Are you going to help me?"

TWO

Superstar Rescue

JUDD stared at Z-Van. He was the lead singer for The Four Horsemen, a man who spat in God's face every time he sang. Young people worshiped him, dressed like him, memorized his lyrics, and imitated his twisted lifestyle.

Judd glanced out the back door. Why did God allow this man to live and Kasim to die? Judd thought.

"Get this stuff off me!"

Judd tried to lift the table, but it wouldn't budge. He checked Z-Van's legs for bleeding. "I have to get something. Hang on."

"Don't leave me!" Z-Van yelled, but Judd scampered outside and found a piece of lumber and wedged it under the table. It moved a few inches.

"Pull yourself out," Judd said.

Z-Van screamed in pain, but he couldn't move his legs.

Judd let the weight settle. He bent to catch his breath and put his hands on his knees. "How did you get the name Z-Van?"

"Look, I'll give you an autograph after you get me out of here."

"I don't want your autograph."

Z-Van shrugged. "Sounded hip at the time. Anything's better than Myron."

"Your real name's Myron? What's your last name?"

"I'll tell you that when my legs are out from under this table." Z-Van looked around the room. "I'm thirsty. Anything to drink around here?"

Judd turned on the faucet and dirty water trickled out.

"No way I'm drinking that stuff."

Judd rummaged through the refrigerator and found a bottle of water. Z-Van drank it and threw the empty bottle in the corner. "I shouldn't have agreed to this gig. The promoter said it was good publicity."

"Most people got out through the front, right?"

"It was awful. Building starts shaking, things flying off the walls, people screaming, climbing over each other. The owner took me the back way and—"

"What's wrong?"

Z-Van tried to sit up. "The owner was right beside me when this came down."

Judd crawled behind the table and noticed a man's shoe sticking out of the rubble. Z-Van shuddered and tried to move away. "I have to get out of here. Just do what you have to."

Judd walked out the back and heard a GC public-address truck in the distance asking for volunteers. He had to find someone to help him pull Z-Van out.

Vicki and the others watched the news reports the rest of the morning. Many areas of Jerusalem had hardly any damage, while the east side looked like a bomb had exploded. Cameras captured collapsed apartment buildings and roads that had become chunks of upturned asphalt and mud.

The death toll was first announced in the hundreds, but only a few minutes later estimates climbed into the thousands. Leon Fortunato hastily called a press conference and spread out a sheet of paper in front of him. He pursed his lips and grimaced.

"I have just come from a meeting with Potentate Carpathia about the situation on the east side. First, let me say that all delegates to the Gala should still attend the final ceremony tonight. It will be abbreviated.

"The potentate is involved in the search-and-rescue operation, but he asked that I extend his heartfelt condolences to all who have suffered loss."

"I'll bet he's involved," Conrad said. "The guy's probably watching from his hotel."

Fortunato quoted Carpathia as saying, " 'Reconstruction begins immediately. We will not be defeated by one defeat. The character of a people is revealed by its reaction to tragedy. We shall rise because we are the Global Community.

" 'There is tremendous morale-building value in our coming together as planned. Music and dancing will not be appropriate, but we shall stand together, encourage each other, and dedicate ourselves anew to the ideals we hold dear.' "

Fortunato folded the paper and looked at the camera. "Let me add a personal word. It would be most encouraging to Potentate Carpathia if you were to attend in over-whelming numbers. We will commemorate the dead and the valor of those involved in the rescue effort, and the healing process will begin."

When Fortunato finished, Mark reported that thousands had logged on to the kids'

Web site in the past hour. Vicki asked if there was any news from Judd or Lionel, and Mark shook his head.

Lionel pointed to a street in shambles, and Sam followed him into the death zone. Rescue workers hadn't reached the collapsed buildings yet, so Lionel and Sam searched for anyone they could help.

A man with blood streaming down his face limped along. Lionel reached out to help, but the man pulled away. Smoke rose from a few fires that had started. Lionel knew that if gas lines ignited, the whole block could explode.

From across the street came a familiar voice. "Lionel! Sam! Help!"

Lionel ran toward Judd and embraced him. "I thought you were dead."

"Close," Judd said.

"Did you find Kasim?"

Judd nodded. "He didn't make it."

"What?" Lionel said. He leaned against the roots of an upturned tree and ran a hand through his hair.

"There's no time to mourn now," Judd said. "There's a guy trapped in back."

Judd led them through the front of the

building and into the narrow passage in the ceiling. "If we get him out from under the rubble, we'll have to find another way to get him to one of the rescue trucks."

"Who is it?" Lionel said.

"See for yourself."

Lionel knelt near Z-Van, and his mouth formed an O.

"Good, you found somebody to help," Z-Van said. "Hurry up!"

Sam ran to find another way out while Judd and Lionel worked on Z-Van. Lionel lifted the table a few inches while Judd tried to pull the man away from the debris. Judd almost had him out when the board snapped and the table fell on Z-Van's feet with a sickening crunch. The singer screamed in pain. Lionel put his fingers under the table and lifted with all his might until Judd pulled Z-Van away.

Lionel collapsed, wheezing and coughing. Z-Van's boots were covered with dust and his legs were twisted. They tried to make him comfortable, but the pain was so great that Z-Van moaned and cried.

Judd waved Lionel to the back door and showed him Kasim's body.

"Doesn't seem fair, does it?" Lionel said.

"That's what I thought. What should we do about Kasim's body?"

"No way we're getting it out of here by ourselves. Let's get this guy out of here and go tell Kasim's parents."

Sam rushed back, excited about finding a way to the street. Lionel rummaged through debris and found a board big enough to use as a stretcher. There was so much rubble that the three had to stop several times before reaching the street. Judd waved at a rescue truck, but it was already full.

"Tell them who I am!" Z-Van shouted.

"I don't think they care," Lionel said.

"Let's take him back to the General's house," Sam said. "He'll know a doctor."

"Take the key from my pocket," Z-Van moaned. "I have painkillers in my hotel room."

Judd took the key and noticed it was from the same hotel Carpathia and his potentates were using. Judd asked Sam to phone the General's driver and meet them a few streets outside the quake zone.

Judd and Lionel carried Z-Van to the meeting place. By the time they made it, Sam was there and Z-Van had passed out.

"The driver is on his way," Sam said. "General Zimmerman says they will have a bed ready and he's calling a doctor he knows."

"Good," Judd said, slipping the key back

into Z-Van's pocket. "I don't want to go to that hotel room. We probably wouldn't be able to get by security anyway."

"What about Kasim's parents?" Lionel said as the limousine pulled up.

"Let's get this guy to Zimmerman's; then we'll find them."

Lionel noticed people walking toward the closing ceremony site and shook his head. "I can't believe they're going through with it."

"You know Carpathia," Judd said. "They'll throw this party even though millions have died. What's a few more thousand to them?"

Judd was surprised to find General Zimmerman's home almost empty. Mr. Stein and the other witnesses were still at the earthquake site helping victims.

Sam, Lionel, and Judd carried Z-Van into the house and placed him on a bed. He awoke and screamed for his pills. General Zimmerman ushered an older man into the room and led Judd and the others into the living room.

"The doctor is a neighbor a few houses away. He is not a believer . . . yet." The General smiled. "He is very good. He will help the young man."

Judd explained who Z-Van was and where they had found him. When he gave the news about Kasim, the General looked troubled. "We should find his parents quickly. They are helping with the rescue operation."

The General left the room to make a phone call to Mr. Stein while Judd flipped on the latest news. Aerial shots of Jerusalem showed that about a tenth of the Holy City had been destroyed.

"Early estimates of the dead have been changed," a reporter said. "It now appears, according to Global Community sources, that the death toll could rise to as many as seven thousand by tomorrow morning."

"And they're still going ahead with the closing ceremony," Lionel said. "Unbelievable."

"One other note," the reporter continued. "One of the most popular performers at the Gala, Z-Van of The Four Horsemen, was making an appearance in the quake zone at the time of the disaster and is feared dead."

"Should we tell them he's all right?" Sam said.

"Not yet," Judd said. "We don't want the GC coming here."

General Zimmerman returned and said Mr. Stein had lost contact with Kasim's parents. Judd called Yitzhak's house, but there was no answer.

"What about Kasim's apartment?" Lionel said.

"I don't think they know where it is, but I'll check," Judd said. "You and Sam go back and look for them in the death zone."

Before Judd left, he checked Z-Van. The doctor reported that he was resting comfortably. "We won't know about his legs until I take him to my office for X rays. We're going there now."

Judd told General Zimmerman their plan and the man nodded. "Take my cell phone and let me know if you find Kasim's parents. Will you be going near the Gala?"

"Kasim's apartment is located near the main stage."

"Be careful, and see if you can spot my friend Chaim Rosenzweig."

"I thought he was sick."

"He's made a miraculous recovery! He'll be in a wheelchair, but I'm told he will sit on the main stage behind Carpathia!"

Judd walked into the street just as the sun moved from behind a cloud. The orange glow made the old city look beautiful—and yet, Judd knew this was another tragic day. They had lost another believer and friend, and thousands lay crushed under the rubble only a short distance away.

Judd thought about the Gala. Would this be the night Carpathia was killed? Would the brilliant Chaim Rosenzweig keep turning from God and follow Carpathia? And what if Judd found Jamal and Lina, Kasim's parents? How could he tell them of the death of their only son? Judd thought of Z-Van. He wanted to talk to the man about the truth, but he seemed so far away from God.

The sun warmed Judd as he walked closer to Kasim's place. People in the streets weren't dancing or drinking now. They soberly moved toward the man they thought had answers to their problems.

But Judd knew something they didn't. According to the Bible, Satan himself would soon inhabit Carpathia.

THREE

Murder by Sword

JUDD squeezed through the massive crowd
and followed a couple into Kasim's building.
The apartment wasn't locked and Judd
walked in, hoping to find Kasim's parents.
They weren't there.

Judd closed the door and sat in front
of the window. Using Kasim's binoculars, he
saw the ornate stage with a row of chairs set
up behind the lectern. A man in a wheelchair was taken to the right just below the
stage.

That must be Dr. Rosenzweig, Judd
thought. He wondered if any of the members
of the adult Tribulation Force were in the
audience. But who could tell? A sea of people
waited patiently for their leader.

A guard searched Dr. Rosenzweig. Then
four men lifted the chair to the stage and

rolled him to his place at the end of the row.
Dr. Rosenzweig playfully drove the motor-
ized wheelchair back and forth across the
stage. The crowd, which had been quiet,
began to respond to the old man, smiling
and laughing.

Lionel and Sam searched for Mr. Stein, but
hundreds of rescuers were in the streets looking for survivors. GC helicopters buzzed the
tops of buildings, and on every corner emergency vehicles waited for the injured. Lionel
overheard a radio transmission from a hospi-
tal saying it was closed to new patients. A
nearby school had been set up as a tempo-
rary morgue.

Sam waved at one of the Jewish believers
staying at General Zimmerman's house, and
the man approached. "I believe God placed
us here at this critical time," the man said.
"I have prayed with three people since the
earthquake."

As the sun set, Lionel and Sam returned to
the music store to check on Kasim's body.
No one had discovered him, so Lionel and
Sam found two pieces of metal and began to
dig. By nightfall they had pulled Kasim's

body away from the rubble and wrapped it in a tablecloth Sam found inside.

"You're Jewish," Lionel said. "Don't you have a problem touching a dead body?"

"This is my brother in Christ," Sam said. "I want to make sure his parents are able to say good-bye."

Lionel and Sam carried Kasim's body a few blocks, avoiding GC personnel. General Zimmerman's driver met them and returned to the General's house.

"But we still have to find his parents," Sam said.

Judd watched the potentates climb the stage steps and shake hands with each other. The mood was somber, no music or even an opening prayer. The huge lighting system bathed the plaza in white light.

Judd scanned the crowd with the binoculars, searching for Kasim's parents. The gathering looked even bigger than opening night.

Finally, Leon Fortunato and Nicolae Carpathia mounted the stairs, surrounded by security guards. When the crowd recognized them, they applauded politely. Leon had each of the potentates stand as he introduced them. Then he let Carpathia introduce the final guest.

Vicki and the others in Wisconsin had watched the earthquake coverage all day and waited for word from Judd or Lionel. When Nicolae Carpathia finally stood to quiet the crowd, several kids groaned.

"Let me add my deep thanks to that of our supreme commander's and also my sympathies to you who have suffered," Carpathia began. "Many in the music world mourn tonight because of the death of one of the leading entertainers of our day."

A picture of Z-Van appeared on the huge screens around the plaza and the crowd was silent, except for some who cried and wiped away tears. After a moment of silence, Carpathia continued. "I will not keep you long, because I know many of you need to return to your homelands and are concerned about transportation. Flights are going from both airports, though there are, of course, delays.

"Now before my remarks, let me introduce my guest of honor. He was to have been here Monday, but he was overtaken by an untimely stroke. It gives me great pleasure to announce the miraculous rallying of this great man, enough so that he joins us tonight in his wheelchair, with wonderful prospects for complete recovery. Ladies and gentlemen of the Global Community, a statesman, a scientist, a loyal citizen, and my dear friend, the distinguished Dr. Chaim Rosenzweig!"

Vicki shook her head as the crowd erupted. "You'd think somebody as smart as Dr. Rosenzweig wouldn't believe Carpathia's lies."

Judd had a perfect view of Dr. Rosenzweig as Nicolae held up the man's good arm in a gesture of victory. The crowd cheered on.

Finally, Nicolae returned to the podium and spoke somberly. "Fellow citizens, in the very young history of our one-world government, we have stood shoulder to shoulder against great odds, as we do tonight.

"I had planned a speech to send us back to our homes with renewed vigor and a rededication to Global Community ideals. Tragedy has made that talk unnecessary. We have proven again that we are a people of purpose and ideals, of servanthood and good deeds."

Three potentates behind Carpathia stood. The other seven rose slowly and clapped. Carpathia turned as the crowd picked up the applause.

That's strange, Judd thought.

The potentates sat and Carpathia hesitated.

He turned and jokingly said, "Do not do that to me."

Judd jumped from his seat, aware that something was about to happen. He bolted from the room, binoculars dangling from his neck, and ran down the stairs. He had to get to the stage.

Vicki and the others wondered what was going on as Carpathia smiled and laughed. The camera switched to the potentates, three of whom stood again and applauded, as if trying to score points with Nicolae. The audience chuckled and applauded again.

"Look, Dr. Rosenzweig's doing his wheelchair routine again," Conrad said.

It was true. Rosenzweig wheeled himself toward Leon Fortunato as the crowd continued clapping. The camera panned the crowd. Everyone was on their feet now, raising their hands, shouting, and jumping.

"I wish we could cut to Vicki B. right now," Mark said.

Vicki nodded. "I'd love a chance to speak to this crowd."

Suddenly, an explosion rocked the festivities, and the camera went out of control. The kids all sat forward, trying to see what had happened.

Judd raced for the stage, but people stood shoulder to shoulder. Security guards had cleared people from trees surrounding the plaza, but Judd took a chance and put one foot on a tree trunk and jumped as high as he could, barely reaching the lowest branch. He pulled himself up and sat, trying to orient himself. One of the speaker stands was only ten feet away, so Judd could hear every breath from Carpathia.

Judd put the binoculars to his eyes just as a guard below shouted at him. Judd ignored the man and saw that he had a perfect view of the stage from the same angle as before.

"I said come down from there now, or—"

A gunshot exploded to Judd's right. The lectern shattered, and the huge curtain behind Carpathia ripped away. Judd turned to see who had fired the shot, but something silver caught his eye at the back of the stage. At first, Judd thought it was Chaim Rosenzweig's wheelchair, but as he looked closer, he saw Chaim holding a sword.

Carpathia reeled from the shot, stumbled, and fell backward toward Chaim. Judd gasped as Dr. Rosenzweig lifted the sword to meet the potentate. The blade plunged into his head, and Carpathia's hands shot to his chin. Chaim twisted the handle of the sword and let go. The potentate rolled to the stage floor and Chaim steered to the left, away from the body.

Judd kept his eyes on the platform as chaos broke out all around him. Dr. Rosenzweig seemed puzzled, like he was having another stroke. The other potentates scurried off the back of the stage and jumped to the ground.

The crowd screamed and ran away. Some at the front ducked under the stage. Others ran for safety and trampled those who were slower. A few climbed up the tree Judd was in and sat on other branches.

Dr. Rosenzweig moved his wheelchair to the rear of the stage and rolled out of the chair. To Judd's amazement, he tossed his blanket over the side, threw his feet over the edge, and disappeared behind the stage.

How did he do that? Judd thought.

Judd focused on Carpathia. The most powerful man on the face of the earth lay in a pool of blood. From the nearby speaker tower, Judd heard Carpathia gasp and speak a few words. "But I thought . . . I thought . . . I did everything you asked," he choked.

Leon Fortunato leaned over Carpathia's body, fell upon the potentate's chest, and pulled his body up into an embrace. The audio cut out as Leon rocked Carpathia back and forth. Judd looked closely and thought he saw Carpathia's lips move again. The nearby speaker crackled, and Judd heard the man say, "Father, forgive them, for they know not what they do."

Fortunato wailed, "Don't die, Excellency! We need you! The world needs you! *I* need you!"

People stampeded the plaza in a human tidal wave. Judd noticed a scaffold swaying as people ran by. Three stories up, the giant speakers leaned under the stress of the torrent. Suddenly, a ten-foot-square speaker box teetered. Judd instinctively shouted, but no one heard him. The speaker snapped its moorings and fell, landing on a woman. A man tried to drag her body from under the smashed speaker, but people around him pushed him out of the way and the crowd kept running.

Vicki shuddered as she and the others watched the replay of the assassination. The news anchors were almost speechless as they replayed video showing the lectern splintering and the curtain taking the impact of the bullet. Carpathia fell and the dignitaries onstage scurried away.

"I didn't think it was supposed to be a gunshot," Conrad said.

"Tsion thought it would be a sword," Mark said. "Guess he was wrong."

Lionel and Sam arrived at the Gala seconds after the shot had been fired. As thousands screamed and fled the scene of the assassination, Lionel and Sam inched toward the stage, unaware of what had happened.

As they came closer, Lionel saw Carpathia on the platform, his wrists drawn under his chin, his eyes shut. Blood trickled from his mouth and ears and he shook violently.

Leon Fortunato screamed, "Oh, he's gone! He's gone! Someone do something."

A helicopter landed and emergency medical personnel hopped out. Some rushed to Carpathia, while others tended to those who had been trampled in the plaza and to a woman who had been crushed by a falling speaker.

Emergency workers tried to help Carpathia, but it looked like gallons of blood had pooled from his wound. Lionel noticed Mac McCullum making his way up the steps.

Fortunato screamed and pushed his way between the medical personnel. He knelt in

Nicolae's blood and buried his face in the man's lifeless chest. Another man gently pulled Leon away from the body, and the two talked for a moment.

GC guards surrounded the stage, holding high-powered weapons. Lionel tugged on Sam's arm and the two left.

"Who do you think did it?" Sam said.

"Doesn't matter," Lionel said. "They'll come after followers of Ben-Judah with a vengeance."

When Judd finally made it back to General Zimmerman's home, he found Lionel and Sam in the entryway. They took him aside and told him what they had done with Kasim's body.

"Kasim's mom and dad just got here," Lionel said. "They're waiting in the meeting room."

Judd found the two sitting, Mr. Stein kneeling before them in prayer. "Do they know?" Judd whispered to Lionel.

"Not yet."

When Mr. Stein had finished his prayer, Judd sat beside them and told them the whole story. Jamal and Lina asked to see Kasim's body, and Lionel showed them.

Judd wept with Kasim's surviving family members, thinking of Nada and all his other friends who had died. He longed for the Glorious Appearing of Christ, but he knew that was three and a half years away.

FOUR

Z-Van's Decision

JUDD found something to eat and watched the news coverage at General Zimmerman's house. He was exhausted but couldn't sleep. He asked about Z-Van and learned the man had hairline fractures in both legs and feet.

"The doctor sedated him and put casts on," Lionel said. "He's asleep in one of the guest rooms."

"Does anyone know he's alive?"

"He told the doctor he didn't want anyone to know. Said he wanted to see how the media would cover his death."

Judd shook his head. "All those people killed in the earthquake and this guy thinks about publicity."

A grieving Supreme Commander Leon Fortunato appeared at a live news conference. He had changed from his bloodstained clothes and looked sad.

"As the news media has already reported, I now confirm the death of our beloved leader and guide. We shall carry on in the courageous spirit of our founder and moral anchor, Potentate Nicolae Carpathia. The cause of death will remain confidential until the investigation is complete. But you may rest assured the guilty party will be brought to justice."

"They don't know who did it," Judd said.

"You mean who shot him?" Lionel said.

"He wasn't shot. It was a sword, just like Tsion said." Judd explained what he had seen to Lionel.

Lionel said, "But Dr. Rosenzweig has been very ill. How could he have done such a thing and escaped?"

"He must have been faking it," Judd said.

A news anchor said the body of the slain potentate would lie in state in the New Babylon palace before entombment Sunday. Judd looked at Lionel and swallowed hard. "When do you think it will happen?"

Lionel pursed his lips. "Sometime in the next two days. And then Carpathia is going to be even more evil than he has been, if that's possible."

Sam ran into the room and tapped Judd's shoulder. "Z-Van's awake. He wants to see you."

As the assassination coverage continued,
Vicki gathered everyone. Some of the kids
knew as much as Vicki, but Janie and
Melinda were new to the Bible.

Janie scratched her head. "You guys really
think Carpathia is coming back from the dead?"

"Tsion Ben-Judah thinks so," Vicki said,
grabbing a Bible. "Everyone was surprised
about Eli and Moishe, but listen to this." She
turned to Revelation 11. " 'But after three and
a half days, the spirit of life from God entered
them, and they stood up! And terror struck all
who were staring at them. Then a loud voice
shouted from heaven, "Come up here!" And
they rose to heaven in a cloud as their enemies
watched.' "

"Does it say anything about the earthquake?" Janie said.

"It says an earthquake will destroy a tenth
of the city."

"Wow," Janie said. "So it says Carpathia is
going to come back from the dead too?"

"Revelation talks about the beast—and we
think that's Carpathia—receiving a mortal
wound. He later ascends from the bottomless
pit, so we think that means he'll come back to
life."

"Couldn't he just indwell Fortunato?" Mark said.

"Yeah, but Satan loves to counterfeit what God does." Vicki pointed to the television. "And you can bet, if Carpathia does come back to life, they'll have the replay going 24/7."

"Wait," Conrad said. "Dr. Ben-Judah was wrong about his sword prediction. The reports say he was shot."

"I don't have a good answer for that," Vicki said.

"When he comes back to life, will he be the same guy or somebody different?" Melinda said.

"His body will be the same, and I assume his voice will be too, but there will be a big difference inside because of the indwelling."

Melinda scowled. "What does *indwelling* mean?"

Mark raised a hand. "It'll be the same bus, different driver."

"I still don't get it," Janie said.

"*Indwell* means to live inside," Vicki said. "Satan is going to live inside Nicolae's body."

Janie shivered and rubbed her arms. "You mean, like possession? I saw a scary movie once about a kid who talked in weird voices."

"Same thing," Vicki said, "only this is the ultimate possession."

Vicki glanced at the television and saw a group of children marching toward a picture of Nicolae Carpathia.

"It's video from one of those staged rallies," Mark said.

The children, most of whom were two to three years old, were dressed in cute GC outfits. When they reached the platform, they saluted and sang a short song of praise to Carpathia. Several laid flowers below the picture. Vicki turned up the volume as the children knelt and began a prayer. "Our Father in New Babylon, Carpathia be your name. Your kingdom come, your will be done. . . ."

Vicki shook her head and hit the mute button.

Shelly said, "I can't believe they brainwashed little kids like that."

"It's going to get worse," Vicki said. "Satan is drawing as many followers as he can. God is extending mercy to anyone who will follow him. It's a huge battle."

"Did people before the Rapture believe all this would happen?" Conrad said. "Nobody ever talked to me about it."

"I don't know," Vicki said. "The point is, we have to do everything we can to help people know the truth."

"Back to this indwelling thing," Melinda said. "When's it going to happen?"

"The Bible doesn't say. But I know a lot more people are going to believe Carpathia's lies after it does."

The television blared as Judd sat by Z-Van's bed. Pillows propped the man's legs, and he winced when Judd put a hand on the bed.

Judd wanted to tell the truth about God, but he could put their group in danger if Z-Van told the authorities what was going on in General Zimmerman's home.

Z-Van broke the silence. "Real bummer about what happened to the big guy, huh? I'd like to get my hands on whoever fired the gun."

Judd nodded. "How are you feeling?"

"Like I've still got a thousand pounds on my legs." Z-Van turned down the volume on another replay of the assassination. "I want to thank you—you and your friends. I can be pretty demanding; that's what my band members say. You did a good thing for me, and I want to return the favor."

"You don't need to—"

"I know, but if you hadn't come along, I might still be there."

"Somebody from your band would have found you."

Z-Van laughed. "Those guys were probably partying."

Judd changed the subject. "You never told me your real last name."

"Is that what you want?"

"I told you, I don't want anything for helping you."

Z-Van took a sip of ice water and pushed hair from his face. "Vanzangler. Myron Vanzangler. You call me Myron in front of your friends and I'll kick you with these casts."

Judd smiled. "So you switched the *Z* and the *van* around and became Z-Van?"

"Something like that." Z-Van grabbed a cigarette, lit it, and blew smoke toward the ceiling.

"Lionel said you didn't want anyone to know you were alive."

"Lionel—is that the black kid?"

Judd nodded.

"Where are you guys from?"

"A suburb of Chicago."

"You're a long way from home." Z-Van cursed, grabbed a pencil, and scratched underneath his cast. "I figure I'll pull a McCartney. Back in the 1960s, they put out records and stories that the guy was dead when he wasn't. Great promotion. Sales shot up and everybody wondered what happened. I'll do the same thing, and the Global Community will help."

"How?"

"I lay low for a few days, figure out a good time to come back from the dead, and voila, I'm bigger than ever."

"If that's the way you want to play it," Judd said.

"You don't think it will work?"

"Maybe it will. But what if your fans get ticked? You're fooling them."

"How would you play it?"

Judd thought a moment. "Tell them the truth. Fast. You were trapped in the earthquake, you got help, and as soon as you're better you'll be back onstage."

Z-Van shook his head. "No pizzazz. You gotta be more creative." He closed his eyes. "Okay, how about this? I stay gone for a year, work on some songs and let my legs heal; then I come back with a tour that'll rock their socks."

"I still think your fans will be upset. Somebody's going to see you, and the media will plaster your face all over the news."

Z-Van scratched his chin. "Hand me the phone."

Judd gave it to him and Z-Van dialed a number. "Westin Jakes' room?" He paused. "Wes, it's me. . . . No, just listen. I don't want anybody to know, all right? . . . Yeah, I figured you'd try. Where's the plane? . . . Good. Meet me there—" Z-Van put his hand over the phone. "What day is it?"

"It's past midnight . . . Saturday morning."

"Okay, have the plane ready early this afternoon. . . . No, don't file a flight plan; this is a secret. . . . Yeah, I'll have somebody with me, but not from the band."

Z-Van talked a few moments more, then hung up. "Wes is the only one I trust out of the bunch. He said he'd have the plane ready for us."

"Us?"

"Yeah, you need a ride back home, right? That's the least I can do for somebody who saved my life."

"But—"

"We'll talk tomorrow. Let me get some sleep."

Judd's mind reeled as he joined the others. Could God be providing a way home through this ungodly man?

New believers lined the walls of the meeting room and spilled into the hall. Mr. Stein called for quiet as Judd found Sam and

Lionel and whispered what Z-Van had said to him.

Mr. Stein prayed, then said, "I believe we are in grave danger. If any of you wish to leave, now is the time."

"Why are we in danger?" a man in a long robe said.

"With the death of Nicolae Carpathia, the Global Community will have every reason to go after their enemies. I believe they will come after followers of Tsion Ben-Judah. It could mean imprisonment or perhaps our lives."

"What will you do?" another man asked.

"I met many of you at the earthquake site. It was there that you acknowledged the true God of heaven and his only Son, Jesus, the Messiah."

Men and women raised hands and shouted praise to God. Some fell to their knees and worshiped.

Mr. Stein allowed them a few minutes, then continued. "As you can see, these new believers have a great passion for the God who delivered them. I think they will be used by him in the next few days."

A young man whose clothes had been torn spoke. "I would give my life to proclaim the news that Jesus is the true Potentate. I want my family and friends who are still alive to hear the truth!"

Others shouted in agreement and praised God. General Zimmerman went through the crowd, explaining to newcomers where they could sleep.

Mr. Stein told the group about Z-Van's condition. A few murmured and Mr. Stein held up a hand. "We will pray that God would bring this man to the truth."

A noise outside startled the gathering. Judd ran to the front door and threw it open. Rolling bullhorns blasted a police report to the neighborhood in various languages. After a few moments of French, and then what must have been Italian, the announcment was finally made in English.

"Attention, citizens and all Global Community personnel! Be on the lookout for American Rayford Steele, former GC employee wanted in connection with the conspiracy to assassinate Potentate Nicolae Carpathia. May be in disguise. May be armed. Considered dangerous. Qualified pilot. Any information about his whereabouts will be rewarded by the Global Community. . . ."

Judd couldn't believe it. Rayford Steele didn't kill Carpathia, but the GC was charging him with the crime. Someone turned up the sound on the television, and Rayford's official GC photo flashed on the screen.

The news anchor smiled. "This should end any doubt about the ability of the Global Community to track down the killer. I repeat, fingerprints on the weapon found near the stage where Potentate Carpathia was shot and killed tonight are those of former Global Community employee Rayford Steele. Our sources tell us that from the different camera angles they have, Rayford Steele fired on the Potentate and sent the world into a state of mourning."

The anchor questioned a GC crime expert and asked if the shooting might be a conspiracy. "Our source tells us Steele is a committed Judah-ite," the expert said. "At this point, anything is possible."

Judd got everyone's attention and told them the details of what he witnessed there and who had really killed Nicolae Carpathia.

"So it was a sword," Mr. Stein said, "just as Tsion predicted."

Someone shouted from the kitchen area, and everyone ran to the back of the house. Judd pushed his way through and gasped. Chaim Rosenzweig's house was engulfed in flames.

FIVE

Change of Plans

JUDD and the others rushed to the Rosenzweig estate, but it was too late. Flames
licked at every level of the home and out the
windows. Soon, the beautiful house would
be nothing but charred rubble.

Global Community officers kept people
back. A television crew set up nearby and
prepared to go live.

"Behind me you see the estate of international statesman and beloved Israeli inventor,
Dr. Chaim Rosenzweig," the young reporter
said. "Dr. Rosenzweig was on the stage
tonight as a special guest of Potentate Carpathia. Authorities fear that after the assassination of His Excellency, Rosenzweig returned
here and was killed in this fire, along with his
staff."

"What?" Judd said to Lionel. "How could
they know that?"

"A Global Community source who asked not to be named gave us information that there are a number of bodies inside, and that there is no possibility of getting them out until the fire has been brought under control."

Judd shook his head and walked back to the General's house. He took Lionel and Sam aside. "Okay, help me figure this out. Rosenzweig kills Carpathia. The GC had to have seen it on the video. They torch his house and kill him, but then they accuse Rayford Steele of killing Carpathia. Why?"

"Maybe they think they can get two people with one assassination," Sam said. "Whether Steele fired the shot or not, they accuse him and all believers will be suspect."

"Do you really think Captain Steele fired the shot?" Lionel said.

Judd was distracted by the television news which again showed Rayford Steele's picture and aired his voice. "This man may be in disguise," the anchor said. "He is considered armed and extremely dangerous. If you see him, contact your local GC post. Again, this man, Rayford Steele, is believed to be the lone assassin, the lone gunman who shot and killled Nicolae Carpathia Friday night. Global Community Security and Intelligence forces found his fingerprints on what is

believed to be the murder weapon, a powerful handgun known as a Saber."

Mr. Stein turned the sound down as the
others came back. Judd asked if he thought
Dr. Rosenzweig could have prayed before he
was killed in the fire.

Mr. Stein shook his head. "I hope he did.
Now, let us pray for the protection of our
brother Rayford Steele."

Lionel met with Judd the next morning after
sending an e-mail to Vicki and the others
back home. He explained all that had happened and asked the kids to pray about their
return to the States.

"How did you sleep?" Lionel said.

"I thought about Z-Van's offer all night."

"You think I could come?"

"That's the only way I would go," Judd
said, "but I don't know. This guy's life is so
messed up. He's into himself and the Global
Community. If he finds out who we are, he'll
probably turn us in."

"He might listen. You don't get trapped
under that much rubble and not think about
God."

"Or we could just keep quiet." Judd looked
in the other room. "What about Sam?"

"He's been with Mr. Stein a lot. He might want to stay here, but let's ask him if he wants to go to the States with us."

Vicki relayed Lionel's message, and the kids were astonished at what Judd and Lionel had seen. Everyone grieved the loss of Kasim and watched reports of the mounting death toll in Jerusalem. Nearly seven thousand had died according to the GC CNN reports. Mark took Lionel's e-mail, cut references to Chaim Rosenzweig and other people, and composed an "eyewitness report" from Jerusalem.

Vicki knew readers of the kids' Web site expected timely reporting. The response to Mark's article came immediately.

Thank you for preparing us, one girl wrote from Cleveland. *I've been watching the coverage nonstop and trying to tell my friends what's about to happen, but they don't believe me. Your article convinced one friend and she just prayed with me. Keep up the good work.*

Hundreds of messages came in all evening, and Vicki alternated between the television and the computer. Late that evening the kids agreed to take turns watching TV to make sure they didn't miss Carpathia's resurrection. Mark and Conrad took the first shift.

Vicki fell asleep quickly and was awakened after midnight by Darrion. "We're up."

Vicki poured them both a cup of coffee and they sat on the floor, afraid they would fall asleep on the couch. Vicki always loved the smell of coffee but didn't like the taste much. Now the bitter taste stung her tongue and she hoped it would keep her awake.

The news carried video of Nicolae Carpathia's plane landing in New Babylon. An honor guard reverently carried the casket into the airplane hangar. As they watched the round-the-clock coverage, Vicki asked Darrion if she wanted to talk about her bad memories of the summer home.

Darrion nodded and put her coffee on an end table. "I guess I'm ready. Like I told you before, I was mad at my parents, so I wanted to hurt them for not paying attention to me. I got together with a girlfriend of mine. Her brother and another guy drove us. I stole the house key from my dad's key ring."

As Darrion talked, Vicki felt uneasy, but she kept her composure and didn't overreact. "You've never told anybody?"

Darrion shook her head. "My friend Stacey passed out on the couch. When I told her later, she didn't believe me. I never told anybody else."

"How old were the guys?"

"Her brother was seventeen, the other fifteen. I was about thirteen."

"Do you want to tell me what happened?" Vicki said.

Darrion took a breath. "Stacey passed out from too much beer or too much weed, and the guys started talking to me. They were nice at first."

Darrion's lip quivered, and Vicki put an arm around her. "Something changed and I could tell it. I told them to back off and they laughed. I punched Stacey and tried to wake her up, but she was out cold.

"I ran to the kitchen. I remembered a lady coming to our school saying never be alone with strangers like this, but it was too late. I never thought it could happen to me."

"They ran after you?"

"They were right behind me in the kitchen, so I ran out the back door and into the woods. I'd taken my shoes off, so the rocks and sticks hurt my feet. I heard them behind me, laughing. One of them had a flashlight. I tried to hide, but I was breathing so loud they found me."

Darrion stood and walked to the front window, her back to Vicki. The moon was bright and lit the hillside with an eerie glow.

"I've heard that something like one out of

every four women will be hurt like that in their lifetime," Vicki said.

"Yeah, well I'm one of those statistics."

With her back still turned, Darrion told Vicki everything she remembered. "Then, when I got back to the house, they were playing cards in the living room with Stacey. Stacey saw my clothes were dirty and asked what I'd been doing outside. Those guys acted like nothing had happened. They didn't even look up."

Vicki hugged Darrion and whispered, "I'm so sorry. They had no right."

"Stacey didn't believe me!"

"Maybe she thought they'd send her brother to jail."

Darrion clenched her teeth. "That's where he belongs."

"What happened after that?"

"I said I had to go home and they took me. Mom and Dad were waiting. I ran past them to my room. They grounded me, took away my riding privileges at the stable for a week, but we never talked about it."

"And you've carried it with you all this time?"

Darrion nodded, her eyes wet. "That's when I really got into Enigma Babylon One World Faith. I thought I could clear my mind of what happened, focus on the positive, and everything would be all right. But it led me nowhere. I still had all the bad feelings. That's when I met your friend Ryan and he told me about God."

"But you still haven't been able to forget about it, right?"

Darrion shook her head. "I know God loves me and everything, but it still seems like my fault!"

Vicki hugged Darrion again as the girl wept. "You made some bad choices, but what those guys did was wrong." Vicki took Darrion's face in both hands. "That was not your fault."

Darrion cried on Vicki's shoulder. When she had settled down, Vicki broke away and woke Shelly and Janie, telling them it was their turn to watch television.

"Our time's not up," Darrion said.

"It's okay," Vicki said. She grabbed a flashlight and opened the back door. "Take me to where it happened."

Judd spoke with Mr. Stein about Z-Van's offer. Mr. Stein scratched his head and sat back. "This man is living an ungodly lifestyle. He is not trustworthy. He may say one thing and do another. But perhaps this is a way for you to get back to your friends."

"I've been thinking about Z-Van becoming a believer," Judd said. "He's known everywhere."

Mr. Stein smiled. "That would be wonderful, but be careful. Remember the passage that talks about God using the weak things of the world to confound the wise? We must keep preaching the truth about Jesus Christ. We point people to him, whether Z-Van believes the message or not."

Judd slipped into Z-Van's room and found him sleeping.

When Judd turned, Z-Van called to him and tried to sit up. "Do you know how hard it is to lie on your back all night, your legs covered with this plaster? I need a drink."

"I'll get you some water."

Z-Van cursed. "Don't bother."

Judd hesitated, then took a step toward the bed. "I wanted to talk about your offer. Is it still good?"

"The flight home? Yeah. You want to go, you're in."

"I have a couple of friends who might want to go."

"A package deal, huh? We'll have plenty of room. It'll only be Wes and me. Bring whoever you want."

"When do we leave?"

"As soon as you can get a ride to the airport for us."

Judd looked at his watch. He had a lot to do in a short time.

"Question before you go," Z-Van said. "What kind of place is this?"

"It's a man's house. He used to be a general in the Israeli army."

"Yeah, but I hear people talking, having meetings. What's it about?"

"I'll explain on the plane," Judd said.

Vicki followed Darrion up the hill to a small clearing. The moon was so bright they didn't need the flashlight.

"The brush is thick now, but I think this is where they caught me," Darrion said. She was trembling, her hands clasped tight and her shoulders hunched.

"Okay," Vicki said. She knelt with Darrion, the cold dew quickly seeping through her jeans, making her knees icy. "First I want us to pray."

Vicki began but had to wait for the emotion to pass. "Father, this is the place where something really bad happened to Darrion. You know how much it hurt her. Please, right here, heal Darrion's heart and mind. Help her understand who she is and how much you can help her. In Jesus' name, amen."

Vicki looked at Darrion. "When we get back to the house, I want to show you some verses that talk about how much God loves you. But I brought you out here for another reason.

"Darrion, so many young kids have bad stuff done to them. A lot of them carry that hurt their whole lives and never tell anyone."

"I thought it would go away."

Vicki nodded. "It's scary to tell somebody, and I'm glad you trusted me. I hope it helped."

Darrion bent and pulled some grass, releasing the blades into the breeze. "I still feel like it was my fault."

Vicki took her hand. "You put yourself in a bad place by trying to get back at your parents. You were naïve. But what they did is on them. Nothing justifies that."

Darrion dropped Vicki's hand and stood up, eyeing her. "You seem to know an awful lot about this stuff."

Vicki bit her lip and had to wipe away a tear. "I'm one of those statistics too, Darrion."

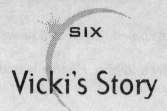

SIX

Vicki's Story

VICKI sat with Darrion on the hillside until the sun came up, telling her own story. It wasn't easy, dredging up painful memories of a trusted uncle who had taken advantage of her when she was only nine.

"And you never told anyone?"

Vicki nodded. "My mom blew me off. Said her brother would never do that and that she would punish me if I ever said anything like that again. So I never did—at least until I was a lot older. When I'd hear my uncle pull up, I'd run and hide."

"Did you feel like it was your fault?" Darrion said.

"Totally. How could I know better?"

"Until . . ."

"Remember us talking about our pastor, Bruce Barnes?"

Darrion smiled. "Ryan said he was incredible."

"I finally told him. He totally understood. He sent me to a woman counselor he trusted."

"Did it help?"

Vicki looked away. "I'd had nightmares. It's always been hard for me to trust guys. The counselor helped me through that. But then Bruce died and we went on the run. I've had other things to worry about ever since."

"Does anybody else know this?"

Vicki shook her head.

Darrion clenched her fists. "I could kill those guys and that uncle of yours."

"I know the feeling, and I won't say it's easy to get past that."

"I don't suppose you can help me find that counselor."

Vicki smiled and looked into her eyes. "I'm no professional, but I'll talk or listen as much as you need."

Judd approached Sam as Lionel packed. When Sam heard about the trip to the States, his eyes widened and then he frowned.

"What's the problem?" Judd said.

"You know how much I would like to go

with you, but I don't feel I can leave Mr. Stein and the others. Something is about to happen here, and I don't want to miss it."

"I understand. How would you feel about the two of us going?"

Sam smiled and looked at the floor. "I consider you my brothers. You helped me understand the truth. I will miss you both."

"We need strong, young believers everywhere. You'll be our main guy in Israel. And if you want to come stay with us, we'll work it out."

Judd phoned Yitzhak's house and reached Kasim's parents. He wanted to speak with them face-to-face, but there wasn't time.

"I keep thinking if I hadn't come here, your daughter and son would still be alive," Judd said, filled with emotion.

"Nonsense," Jamal said. "If it weren't for you, we might never have known Kasim was alive in New Babylon. Go with God. Follow his leading, and we will meet again."

Lina got on the phone to say good-bye. "Don't forget what Nada wrote to you."

Nada's words still haunted Judd. She had sensed there was someone Judd cared about deeply back in the States. Judd could only think of Vicki and was anxious to get home to talk with her.

General Zimmerman said good-bye and offered his limousine to transport them to the secluded airport. Mr. Stein hugged Lionel and Judd, tears in his eyes. "God has used you in miraculous ways, and I pray he will do even more in the future."

Mr. Stein put his hands on their heads and looked toward heaven. "Be gracious to these, your servants, O God. May your face shine upon them and may you give them your peace. Bring others to yourself through their testimony. Amen."

A few of the witnesses carried Z-Van to the limo, and the singer handed them a wad of Nicks, which they all refused. Judd closed the doors and waved good-bye.

His heart was full of emotion as they drove away. So much had happened since they had arrived in Israel. They had lost friends, seen prophecy fulfilled, and witnessed history.

"Who are those people?" Z-Van said as they slowly drove through streets cracked by the earthquake.

Judd turned. Smoke still rose from the rubble of Chaim Rosenzweig's house. Sam Goldberg ran along the street, waving and yelling. Judd and Lionel quickly rolled down their windows and waved.

"They're some of the best friends I've ever had," Judd said to Z-Van.

Vicki awoke with a headache and rushed to see if there was news about Carpathia.

Mark was at the computer, keeping an eye on the coverage and answering e-mails. "I was just going to ask Shelly to get you," he said. "That education guy, Damosa, is supposed to have a special broadcast in a few minutes."

Vicki looked over Mark's shoulder at the new messages. Kids from around the world praised Vicki for her boldness during the GC's satellite transmission. Some wanted more information about how to become a believer.

"There are a few here that look suspicious," Mark said.

He pulled up one from someone who said they lived in Florida. *Hi, Vicki B., I saw you on the satellite feed and think you're really cool. That stuff you said about Jesus is right-on. I'd love to meet with you and your group so I can give you some money to help the cause. Please write back and tell me where we can meet.*

Another from Illinois said: *I heard on television that you live somewhere in Illinois. Or maybe you're not there anymore. Please write*

*me. I have a lot of questions about God, and
I have a safe place to stay if you need one.*

"Move over," Vicki said and she started
typing an answer. "Both of these sound
phony, like they're GC trying to set us up."

"That's what I thought."

Vicki typed: *We know the Global Community
is searching for us. Some of you are offering
money, a safe place to stay, or have questions
about where we are. If you're sincere, thank you.
God is taking care of us. If you're a member of
the Global Community, nice try.*

"Put that on the Web site," Vicki said.

Mark smiled and typed in the Web site
access code. Conrad turned up the sound on
the television. "Your pal's on, Vicki."

An announcer introduced Dr. Neal
Damosa as the leading educator of the
Global Community. He stood in front of a
black shroud, dressed in a stunning outfit, as
usual. The camera zoomed in on his face.

"I have been asked to speak to the young
people of the world and try to make sense
out of what happened in Jerusalem last
night," Dr. Damosa began. "But I can't make
sense of it. Someone, or more likely as we're
hearing from our security forces, a group of
conspirators decided to take the life of our
beloved potentate.

"None of us has words to express the sense

of loss we all feel. In one earth-shattering second, the man who we thought would lead us into a new era of peace and prosperity was taken from us.

"All of the death and destruction we have seen in the last few years could not prepare us for this moment. Most of you have lost fathers and mothers, brothers and sisters, and it may feel at this moment that you have lost another family member."

"Oh, give me a break," Conrad muttered. "Can you imagine having Carpathia as a family member?"

"I'd run away from home," Shelly said.

"In the coming days you will receive instructions about the next round of satellite schools," Damosa continued. "Honor the memory of your fallen potentate. He died in the cause of peace. I urge you to serve the Global Community as he did.

"This is not the end of our dream. It is the beginning. Together we can make the hope of Nicolae Carpathia a reality. It is what he wanted for all of us."

Mark asked Vicki to come to the computer.

"Let me finish—"

"You'll want to see this. It just came in."

Vicki read an e-mail from the pastor in

Arizona she had met on her trip west. The
message was marked "urgent."

> *Vicki and the others of the Young Tribula-*
> *tion Force,*
>
> *A fire was set at the home of Jeff Williams*
> *and his father. Sadly, both died in the fire.*
> *As you know, they were both believers and*
> *growing strong. We can at least be thankful*
> *for that.*
>
> *I have been told that the Global Commu-*
> *nity knows about our meeting place and*
> *that there may be arrests soon. Please pray*
> *for us. The Global Community will stop at*
> *nothing to ferret out the leaders of any who*
> *oppose them.*
>
> *Be on your guard at all times as you con-*
> *tinue to tell the truth boldly.*

Vicki sat back and put a hand to her head.
Jeff Williams and his father were dead? It
seemed like yesterday that she was trying to
explain the gospel to Jeff. Now they were
gone. She sat the others down and told them
Jeff's story. Everyone was saddened by the
news of two more deaths, and they prayed for
the safety of the other believers in Tucson.

"I wonder if Buck knows," Shelly said after
a few moments.

Mark clicked a few keys on the computer. "I don't know if this is related, but Chaim Rosenzweig's home was destroyed by fire last night in Jerusalem."

"How could it be related?" Vicki said. "Unless . . ."

"You think he's become one of us?"

"Let's keep an eye out for other suspicious fires," Vicki said. "This may be the way the GC will try to get rid of believers."

"I've got a bad feeling about Charlie," Darrion said. "What if the GC come back and question that farm couple and Charlie makes a mistake?"

"Have we heard from Charlie or the Shairtons since we left?"

Mark searched through e-mails and came up with nothing. He wrote a quick note to Charlie and asked for an update.

Darrion went out of the room and returned with a cell phone from one of the back rooms. "This is my dad's phone for emergencies. If it works, we could call Charlie and make sure everything's okay."

"Is it GC?" Conrad said.

Darrion nodded.

Vicki turned the phone on and got a dial tone. Mark took it away from her. "Don't risk it. Wait and see if we hear anything from him on e-mail."

Vicki looked worried. She hoped they hadn't left Charlie in a trap.

Judd gasped when he saw the inside of Z-Van's plane. It was almost as elaborate as Nicolae Carpathia's. There were video screens along one wall and a huge seating area. Lionel found a computer and asked if he could e-mail their friends.

"Wait until we get in the air," the pilot said, helping Z-Van get settled. He held out a hand. "Westin Jakes. Nice to meet you."

Judd introduced himself and Lionel, and the two buckled in. "I can't believe we're actually going home."

"About that, we need to take a little detour first," Z-Van said.

"What do you mean?" Judd said.

"I've been thinking about what you said about my fans getting ticked off if I pretend to be dead. Wes and I are working on a welcome back party."

"But you said—"

"Don't sweat, Dorothy. I'll get you back to Kansas."

Judd glanced at Lionel and shrugged. As

the plane screamed down the runway, Judd
wondered if he had led them into a trap. Had
Z-Van heard them talking and figured out
who they were?

As they flew over the Israeli countryside,
Judd knew there was only one option. He
had to confront Z-Van with the truth.

SEVEN

Judd's Flight

VICKI stared at the computer, anxious to hear from Charlie. The others watched news coverage from New Babylon. Already people were spilling into the city to pay their respects to the dead potentate.

Darrion turned to Vicki. "Can you explain one more time what you think's going to happen?"

Vicki ran a hand through her hair. "Dr. Ben-Judah wrote about this, and some people disagreed with him about the wound to the head. They thought the Antichrist wouldn't really die, that he would only appear dead. But Tsion says the best interpretation is that Carpathia will really die and his body will be taken over by Satan himself."

"They're probably embalming the body already," Mark said. "He has to be dead. If they're going to put him in an airtight capsule and let people walk past him like they say on the news, there's no doubt he's dead."

"I can't believe all of this is really in the Bible," Janie said.

Darrion turned up the television as Leon Fortunato appeared at a press conference in New Babylon. He mentioned Rayford Steele's name and said a worldwide search was being conducted.

"Are you sure this man is the shooter?" a reporter asked.

"We have conclusive evidence, including fingerprints, that Rayford Steele is the assassin. I might also add that this man is a Judah-ite, which shows how much they believe in their message of love and peace."

"I can't believe Captain Steele would do something like that," Shelly said.

"Maybe they're framing him for it," Conrad said.

Vicki turned to Mark. "Anything from Charlie yet?"

"No, but a message just came in from . . . hey, it's from Lionel."

The kids gathered around the computer.

> *Judd and I are on a flight heading home. You won't believe who we're with. I'll tell you all about it when we get close.*

> *You'll probably hear on the news that*
> *Rayford Steele is the one who killed*
> *Carpathia. Not true. Judd saw the whole*
> *thing and it wasn't Rayford.*
>
> *Write and tell us where you are and how*
> *to get there. We're not sure right now when*
> *we'll get back or where we'll land, but we*
> *can't wait to see you guys.*

From the TV Leon Fortunato spoke in the background. "We are committed to doing everything necessary to bring the person or persons guilty to justice . . . and we will have justice."

Another reporter asked about the delivery of the potentate's body. "Can you tell us anything about the mood in the palace?"

"We are all devastated, as you might expect. To lose not only a world leader but also someone you considered closer than a brother, well, it is difficult.

"There was a great outpouring of emotion among the workers, the soldiers. Everyone involved was overcome with tears, and yet, there is a sense that he would have wanted us to carry on in the Global Community tradition."

A reporter started another question, but Fortunato, overcome with inspiration, held up a hand. "As you will see tomorrow at his memorial service, those of us who worked with him behind the scenes believe this was no mere man. Many around the world can testify to the power of his words. He was able to calm our fears and lift us up, even in terrible days."

Reporters paused, then threw up their hands. Fortunato pointed to a female reporter who said, "Can you give us specifics about the ceremony tomorrow?"

"We understand that more than a million people have already come to New Babylon, and we expect more than double that number. There will be a public procession past the body, the time yet to be determined. As far as the service tomorrow, I believe not a person on the planet should miss it. It will be transmitted to every locale that has access to our satellite feed. We will unveil a work of art that I think would please the potentate. Throughout the day we will allow guests to pass by the coffin to pay their final respects. But the main service will begin at noon and the burial at 2 P.M."

"What time will that be here?" Janie said.

Mark had devised a counter that converted times in different parts of the world to Central time in the United States. "Looks like we'll be getting up early again."

For the first time since meeting Z-Van, Judd fully realized who he was with. This man wasn't an ordinary celebrity who could get a table at a busy restaurant. Z-Van was one of the top ten superstars in the world. People paid hundreds of Nicks to see him perform. This skinny guy with tattoos all over his body and wraparound sunglasses oozed power. He was used to people getting him anything he asked for. Judd had seen him listed as one of the wealthiest men in the world.

As he looked at all the rings in the man's ears, nose, and lips, Judd felt a mix of contempt and admiration. There was no doubt Z-Van was a good showman and business operator, but he had no friends. His life was filled with drinking, partying, and concerts, but it was empty.

Lionel logged on to news outlets around the world. The main story, of course, was reaction to the death of Nicolae Carpathia. In entertainment news, Z-Van's death was at the top.

Other members of The Four Horsemen expressed their shock and sadness. The manager of the group, who had been injured by falling debris, said he was the last to see Z-Van alive. "I was outside the music store when the earthquake started. I tried to get back inside, but it was too late. By the time I located a search crew, we couldn't find his body."

"Yeah, right." Z-Van laughed. "That weasel never gave a thought about anybody but himself. And my bodyguards ran out faster than anyone."

Z-Van flipped through video channels and found a special program highlighting his career. The program played clips of the satellite school performance in Israel.

"That was a weird gig," Z-Van said. "We were probably seen by more people on the planet than at any other concert, but we were still upstaged by that redheaded chick."

Judd stole a glance at Lionel and smiled. "You still haven't told anyone you're alive?"

"The only ones who know are Wes and your group back in Israel. Now tell me who they are and what you guys are up to."

"Why do you think we're up to something?"

Z-Van lit a cigar and blew a huge plume of smoke toward Judd. "I don't know—holding meetings late at night, a bunch of people with long beards who look like those two crazies at the Wailing Wall. I can guess, but why don't you tell me?"

Judd took a deep breath. "Okay, I'll shoot

straight. We're believers in Jesus Christ, followers of Tsion Ben-Judah, otherwise known as Judah-ites. That group back in Israel is made up mainly of Jewish believers who are telling the world that their only hope for peace is to follow the true God."

Z-Van lowered his head and looked over the top of his sunglasses. "You're not serious."

"Dead serious."

Z-Van shook his head. "How did they trick a couple of smart kids like you into believing that junk?"

"We weren't tricked. This is something we chose to do."

"And I suppose you know that Vicki B. character personally."

Judd nodded. He didn't want to give too much away about the Young Trib Force, but he felt honesty was the best approach.

"Well, that puts an interesting spin on the story."

"What do you mean?"

Z-Van put both hands in front of him, like he was spreading out a banner.

" 'World-Famous Singer Kidnapped by Religious Fanatics.' That's probably what the headline will say."

"We didn't kidnap you," Lionel said. "Judd saved your life."

"Yeah, and now you're going to save my soul. Hand me something to write with; this is going to make a good song."

"You've made a career out of bashing believers and making fun of Tsion Ben-Judah," Judd said. "Have you ever thought it might be true?"

Z-Van chuckled, took off his sunglasses, and put the earpiece in his mouth. "All right. Impress me."

Judd asked Lionel to go to the section on prophecies on the kids' Web site. "These things were written about two thousand years ago. Everything from the massive, worldwide earthquake to the one we just had in Jerusalem. The Bible even predicted that seven thousand would be killed in that quake."

Judd showed Z-Van the prophecies about the locusts, the horsemen, and other events of the past three and a half years. "And from what the Bible says, we think Nicolae isn't going to stay dead."

"You guys are crazy. I've seen the video. Carpathia is dead as a stump."

"What if we're right?"

Z-Van waved him off.

"If Eli and Moishe can come back to life, why not—"

"Those two crazies at the Wailing Wall? Carpathia blew them away days ago."

"He doesn't know," Lionel said.

"God raised them from the dead," Judd said. "They went right up into the clouds."

"Wooooo." Z-Van laughed, moving his finger in a circle in the air. "Then why haven't they shown that on the news?"

"I was there," Lionel said. "The GC won't show the replay because they know it'll affect people."

Judd told his story, beginning with where he was at the moment of the disappearances.

When he finished, Z-Van smiled. "So if you and Lionel are such good people, why weren't you taken?"

"Lionel and I knew the truth, but we didn't live it," Judd said. "I was in church as much as anybody, but being in church doesn't make you—"

"I know, doesn't make you a Christian any more than being in a garage makes you a car. Believe me, I've heard it. You probably won't believe this, but I used to go to church when I was a kid too. Stop staring and close your mouths—it's true."

Z-Van pulled himself up in his chair. "Where do you think I got the name The Four Horsemen? They tried to scare me with that stuff when I was a kid."

"Then you know God's trying to get your

attention. He's calling you back. Do you know how much influence you could have on people if you—"

"Hold on," Z-Van said. "I'm not trying to influence anybody for good or bad. I'm trying to make a living."

Judd laughed. "You're not influencing anybody? Do you know how many kids dress like you, get tattoos, sing your lyrics, and get wasted because they think it's cool?"

"What people do is their own business. I'm an entertainer. The way I look at it, I have to take advantage of the popularity I have now because it might not be here tomorrow."

"Who took you to church when you were a kid?" Lionel said.

"My mother. She'd be there every Sunday and Wednesday. My dad took off before I was born."

"Where's your mom now?" Lionel said.

Z-Van slammed his sunglasses on and pointed toward Lionel. "Watch yourself. Keep my family out of this."

"It's a fair question," Judd said.

"I say it's not. Drop it."

"What did your mom think of your band and what you're doing now?"

"Things didn't skyrocket until after . . . what happened. I can tell you she didn't like my style." Z-Van smiled and imitated his mother in a falsetto voice. " 'I'm praying for you, Myron. God's going to get hold of you someday.' She'd send me tapes of radio programs she'd heard and books about how to keep your family together."

Judd remembered reading about Z-Van's stormy relationships with women. He had been married at least three times and was frequently pictured with Hollywood actresses in the tabloids.

"She wasn't real happy with the choices I'd made, but how can you argue with success, right?"

"I'll bet you haven't talked with her in three and a half years," Judd said. "Did something happen between you two that night?"

Z-Van shook his head and squirmed in his chair. "You guys don't quit, do you?" He tried to stand, but fell back in the leather seat. Finally, he sighed and said, "She disappeared three years ago or whatever it was. She'd just sent me a fresh box of stuff on the end times. Said with the world as crazy as it was, it wouldn't be long before Jesus came back and I needed to be ready."

"Did you ever answer her or talk to her about it?" Judd said.

"Didn't need to. I knew what she would say."

"One more question and I'll leave you alone," Judd said. "We've been straight with you. You do the same."

"Shoot."

"Is there any part of you that deep down thinks your mom might have been right?"

Z-Van clenched his teeth. "No. And that's the last I want to talk about it." He touched the intercom button. "How much longer, Wes?"

"We've got about another hour until touchdown in New Babylon."

"What?" Judd said.

"Go to the back of the plane. I don't want to stare at you for another hour."

"But you said—"

"Leave me alone!"

EIGHT

New Babylon
Touchdown

JUDD and Lionel moved to the back of the
plane and talked about their options. Lionel
found a rear exit they could use after touchdown, but they both agreed it was a last
resort.

"What do you think Z-Van's going to do?"
Lionel said.

"He's pretty ticked. He could call the GC
and have them pick us up at the plane."

"The pilot seems reasonable. Let's talk with
him."

Judd peeked inside the door and saw that
Z-Van had fallen asleep. He and Lionel crept
to the main cabin and lightly knocked on the
cockpit door. The pilot unlocked it and
invited them inside.

"Sorry there's no room to sit," Westin said.
"Heard a little of your tiff with the big guy.
Wasn't smart."

"Do you know what's happening once we touch down?" Judd said.

"I called one of the top GC guys Z-Van knows. I explained what had happened and that we wanted to hold a press conference."

"What about us?" Lionel said.

Westin shrugged. "Z-Van didn't give any instructions about you." He radioed the New Babylon tower and reported their position. Judd and Lionel turned to leave, but the pilot stopped them. "You don't really believe Carpathia is coming back, do you?"

"He could have risen already," Lionel said.

Westin shook his head. "I heard most of what you guys said. Intercom was on. I saw the live video of those two guys come back to life. Incredible."

"Will you help us get back home like Z-Van promised?" Judd said.

"I'll do what I can, but he's the boss."

Judd and Lionel quietly made their way to the back of the plane and buckled in. Judd stared out at the New Babylon skyline. The buildings and elaborate gardens and parks that spread throughout the city were a monument to Carpathia.

As they descended, Judd pointed out a huge scaffold and platform at the front of an open area. Already, thousands of people moved toward the spot. Some would no doubt stay there all night to assure themselves a spot in the funeral service.

Lionel pointed to the vehicles with flashing red lights on the airport runway. "Are those for us or Z-Van?"

Judd shook his head as the plane's wheels touched down.

Vicki and the others watched reports that covered every angle of the potentate's demise. There were replays of Carpathia speeches, reactions from celebrities, and live shots from New Babylon that showed the hurried construction of a viewing area where millions were expected Sunday.

Vicki thought of Charlie and Bo and Ginny Shairton in central Illinois. She prayed for Buck Williams, who would no doubt hear soon about the death of his brother and father. And Vicki thought of Judd. She couldn't believe he and Lionel were finally coming home. When Mark had read the e-mail from Lionel, Vicki hadn't been able to concentrate on anything but the first sentence. She'd felt tears coming and had to turn away. She had thought no one had noticed, but later Shelly asked if she was okay and Vicki whispered that she was excited about seeing Judd again.

There was still no word from Charlie, and Vicki had to resist the urge to pick up Mr. Stahley's phone and dial the number.

The TV coverage switched to an airport in New Babylon, where people of every ethnic background were arriving for the funeral. Incoming flights were sold out, but outgoing flights were empty. No one wanted to leave the city at this historic moment.

A family from Africa stopped to express their feelings. "I have been crying ever since we saw the broadcast," the mother said, holding an infant close. "We were all shocked that this could happen to such a great man."

Her husband grabbed the microphone. "I brought my family here to experience the tragedy firsthand. We want to pass by the body, if that is allowed, and kneel before the greatest world leader in history."

A man from China said, "I brought my wife and my two sons to grieve. It is a time of great sadness, more sadness than we have ever known. But I believe there are great days ahead."

Through an interpreter, a Turkish man said, "The world will never see another like him. It is the worst tragedy we will ever face, and we can only hope that his successor will be able to carry on the ideals he put forth."

"Do you believe Nicolae Carpathia was divine in any sense?" the reporter said.

"In every sense!" the man said. "I believe it's possible that he was the Messiah the Jews longed for all these centuries. And he was murdered in their own nation, just as the Scriptures prophesied."

"Talk about bad theology," Conrad said. "That guy is crazy."

Other people were interviewed on the street. Some speculated about who would succeed Nicolae Carpathia.

"No one has been closer to Potentate Carpathia than Leon Fortunato," a Global Community worker said. "I believe the supreme commander can carry the ideals of Nicolae Carpathia forward so that we can fulfill his dreams."

Mark shook his head. "What a bunch of nonsense."

The report switched to Israel. Vicki thought it would be an update on the earthquake. Instead, thousands of people gathered in front of a few men in robes.

"This is the scene in Jerusalem, just a day after the murder of Nicolae Carpathia," the correspondent said. People in the crowd ran forward, fell to their knees, and shouted their dedication to Jesus.

"Look," Shelly shouted, "Mr. Stein is one of the speakers!"

The camera zoomed in on the bearded men for a few seconds, then pulled back. Vicki couldn't hear what Mr. Stein and his friends were saying, but the effect was clear. They were using this pivotal moment to tell people the truth about God.

A religious expert was called on to explain the phenomenon. He said that since the leaders of the Global Community and the One World Faith were dead, Carpathia and Mathews, people would try to fill that gap in many ways. The expert said that people turning to Jesus Christ was a fairly recent craze that began shortly after the vanishings.

"Dr. Ben-Judah created an uproar, particularly among Jews, when at the end of the live, globally televised airing of his views he announced that Jesus the Christ was the only person in history to fulfill all the messianic prophecies, and that the vanishings were evidence that he had already come."

"So why doesn't this expert have the mark of the believer?" Janie said.

"This guy knows his facts, but he doesn't know God personally," Vicki said. "And he's right about people looking for something to

fill the hole Carpathia left in their lives. Tsion says a lot of people will still believe the truth, but many more will follow false teachers."

"How do you know that?" Janie said.

Vicki pulled up the Bible software on the computer and showed Janie Matthew 24:21-24. "It's talking about what we're about to live through."

"I'm not sure I want to hear it," Janie said.

Vicki read the verses aloud. " 'For that will be a time of greater horror than anything the world has ever seen or will ever see again. In fact, unless that time of calamity is short-ened, the entire human race will be destroyed. But it will be shortened for the sake of God's chosen ones.

" 'Then if anyone tells you, "Look, here is the Messiah," or "There he is," don't pay any attention. For false messiahs and false proph-ets will rise up and perform great miraculous signs and wonders so as to deceive, if possi-ble, even God's chosen ones.' "

"So there are going to be people pretend-ing to do miracles?" Janie said.

"Not pretending," Vicki said. "They're going to perform miracles, and a lot of people are going to think they're from God."

Janie shuddered. "This stuff keeps getting worse and worse."

Vicki checked with Mark. There was still no word from Charlie. Vicki slipped the cell phone in her pocket and walked out of the room.

Judd looked out the window as the plane pulled up to a special hangar at the end of the airport. Several GC vehicles with lights swirling drove close.

"Should we make a run for it?" Lionel said.

Before Judd could answer, the pilot walked into the cabin. "You need to help me get him down the stairs to the wheelchair ramp." When Judd and Lionel hesitated, Westin grabbed Judd's arm. "Now."

Judd looked at Z-Van. "Are you turning us in?"

Z-Van rolled his eyes. "You really think they're interested in a couple of crazy kids when their world has fallen apart?"

"They're ready to crack down on anybody who disagrees with them, and they'll start with followers of Ben-Judah."

Z-Van shook his head. "I'm holding a press conference in the terminal; then I'm meeting with one of Fortunato's aides. I'm telling them you guys saved my life."

"No," Judd said. "Leave us out. Somebody might recognize us."

"Watch the leg!" Z-Van said as they placed him on a ramp. He turned to Judd. "Stay in the plane. I'll know more about our schedule and when we'll leave after this meeting."

"You mean you're still going to give us a ride home?" Lionel said.

"That's what I promised, right? You two just have to promise you won't try to 'save me' again."

Judd and Lionel went back inside the plane and turned on the bank of televisions. Each channel aired Global Community news, but from different perspectives. One channel carried world news while another focused on finances. Lionel turned to a channel geared toward younger people. Already several music videos had been produced with images of Carpathia.

A few minutes later they broke into the regular programming for a special report. A tall, balding GC official appeared before a blue curtain. Several reporters had been hastily recruited for the press conference.

"In the midst of some terrible news, we have a ray of sunshine to report," the man said as his name and title flashed on the screen. "It was previously believed that the lead singer for the group The Four Horsemen had been killed in the earthquake in Jerusalem. However, a few minutes ago we discovered that not only is Z-Van alive, but he is also here in New Babylon to pay his respects to the slain potentate."

The network showed a split screen of the press conference and people inside the terminal. When the pilot wheeled Z-Van into the picture, hundreds of people clapped and cheered. Several young people appeared to faint.

Z-Van took the microphone, his eyes shielded by his patented sunglasses. "First, I want to apologize to everyone who thought I was dead. I didn't mean to put you through this, but after I was pulled from the wreckage by a couple of kids, I didn't have a chance to let anyone know.

"I wanted my first public appearance to be here in New Babylon, out of respect for the man who means so much to me and to the whole world."

"Z-Van, how did you first learn of the potentate's death?" a reporter shouted from the back.

"I was in the doctor's office watching the speech on television. When he was shot, I couldn't believe it. I'd give anything to have that man back with us."

"Will you attend the funeral tomorrow?" another reporter said.

"I've just met with one of the supreme commander's aides and they've asked that I participate somehow. I'm honored and if I can help the world express its grief in some way, I'll be glad to do it."

"Who are the young people who helped you escape the earthquake?" a reporter said.

Z-Van smiled. "Just a couple of guys who really don't appreciate my music as much as they should."

Everyone laughed. Another reporter said, "Will they be with you tomorrow?"

Z-Van nodded. "Yes. They'll join us tomorrow."

Judd looked at Lionel. "We have to find a couple of disguises."

Vicki went into an empty room and found the Shairtons' number. She clicked the phone on, dialed, and quickly hung up. She knew she was taking a great risk using Mr. Stahley's phone, but she had to know about Charlie.

She turned the phone on again and dialed. It rang three times, and Vicki nearly hung up before someone picked up and whispered, "Hello?"

"Charlie, is that you?"

"Vicki?"

"Yes. I called to see if you were all right. Why haven't you written us?"

Charlie's voice trembled through the phone line. "Some of those guys came back and asked Bo more questions."

"You mean the GC?" Vicki said.

"Yeah. They matched the tire tracks to the satellite truck."

"Oh no. Get out of there."

"We were packing up to do that when they—"

"What?" Vicki said.

"They're banging on the door."

Vicki heard a noise in the background. Ginny whispered something to Charlie.

"We're in the cellar place, hiding. I'd better not talk."

Vicki heard a clunk, like Charlie put the phone on a shelf. The banging stopped, and then wood and glass crashed. Someone shouted.

"Charlie?" Vicki screamed.

More splintering wood and men yelling. Bo said something that Vicki couldn't understand.

Mark walked into the room and Vicki waved him off. "Something's happening at the farmhouse."

"You used the phone?" Mark said.

Vicki held a finger to her lips.

"It's gonna be okay," Bo said. "They won't find us down here."

Ginny gasped. "What's that? What's dripping?"

"Gasoline!" Bo said.

The phone clunked again. Charlie said, "Vicki, they're going to burn the place down!"

"Get out!" Vicki screamed. "Get out now!!"

The phone crackled and footsteps pounded on the stairs. Vicki heard banging and someone yelled.

Then the phone went dead.

NINE

Meeting Leon

VICKI rushed into the living room and told the others what she had heard. The kids tried to assure Vicki that Charlie would be okay, but Vicki wouldn't listen. "I should never have let him stay."

"It was his decision," Mark said.

"Now we know the GC's tactic against believers," Conrad said. "They burned Jeff Williams's house, Chaim Rosenzweig's, and now the Shairtons'."

"We have to go back and see if they're all right," Vicki said.

"If they made it out of the house, the GC caught them," Mark said.

"Then we have to go back and get them released!"

"How about that Morale Monitor you know?" Shelly said. "Maybe she can help."

"We haven't heard from Natalie since the message she sent about Carl," Mark said.

While he wrote Natalie, Vicki gathered the others and prayed for Charlie, Bo, and Ginny. They pleaded with God to keep them safe.

Judd moved awkwardly in the Middle Eastern clothing he and Lionel were wearing. They had turbans wrapped tightly around their heads. Judd didn't want to take any chance that the GC might recognize them.

The air was hot but dry in New Babylon as the two walked behind Z-Van's wheelchair. Westin led them up a ramp and into a courtyard, where hundreds of employees had gathered to see the private unveiling of Carpathia's glass coffin.

Spotlights made it seem like daylight as they passed a barricade. A GC official brought the small group near the stand where the coffin would be displayed. "You can watch the ceremony from here," the man said.

Z-Van thanked him and turned to Judd. "You can leave if you want."

"We'll stay."

"Carpathia could rise any minute," Lionel whispered.

A live orchestra played a somber song as ten

pallbearers carried in the Plexiglas coffin. Two hundred yards away men and women from around the world mourned openly. Some cried and wailed, throwing hands in the air. Others fell to the ground and ripped their clothes. Young children screamed and cried. Judd wondered whether they were devoted to Carpathia or just frightened by all the noise.

Pallbearers carefully laid the coffin on its stand and backed away. Employees walked up stairs and filed past the potentate's body. Two pallbearers removed the shroud that covered Carpathia and people gasped.

"I'm sure it wasn't easy to prepare the body for this," Z-Van said.

"Maybe that's not the real body," Lionel whispered to Judd. "They could have made some kind of wax replica so people wouldn't see how torn up he was."

Employees wept as they passed the coffin. Some leaned over the velvet ropes for a closer look. Several crossed themselves or bowed in a religious gesture. One GC official fell to his knees and spoke in a foreign language.

Only a few employees remained in line when barricades were withdrawn and the massive crowd slowly moved toward the casket. A GC official approached Z-Van.

"Would you like us to carry you past the potentate?"

"I'd like my friends to carry me," Z-Van said.

"Fine. Please do not lean on the casket as you pass. No flash photography . . ."

Z-Van held up a hand. "Hey, we don't have a camera and I'm not leaning on anything."

The official bowed. "Of course. Proceed."

Judd and Lionel got on either side of the wheelchair, and Westin lifted from the back. They carried Z-Van up the steps to the platform. Judd nearly tripped over his robe but caught himself in time. Z-Van gave him a stern look. "No funny business, okay?"

Judd nodded and noticed three armed guards next to the coffin. He had seen dead bodies before. An uncle had died when he was young and Judd had touched his face. Carpathia looked more pale than anyone he had ever seen in a casket. The body was vacuum sealed, like a tube of tennis balls.

Z-Van snapped his fingers. "I need a pen and some paper."

Westin pulled out a small pilot's log from his pocket, and Lionel handed the singer a pen. Z-Van jotted a few notes, and they moved along the platform as the GC official told those behind them what to do and not do.

"Excuse me, Mr. Z-Van, sir," a young man said once they reached the bottom of the steps.

Z-Van looked at Westin. "Tell them I don't do autographs while I'm mourning."

"Supreme Commander Leon Fortunato would like to see you before you leave," the man said.

Z-Van glanced at Judd. "I think we have time for the supreme commander. We'd be delighted."

Vicki watched the endless line of mourners file past the see-through coffin. Newscasters spoke quietly like announcers at a golf tournament, not wanting to spoil the somber mood.

Mark yelled and the kids ran to the computer. He pulled up a message from Natalie at one of the GC posts in Illinois and read it out loud. *"Saw your message. Don't have much information on C and the Ss. I know they were under suspicion because the tire tracks matched the satellite truck. I'll let you know ASAP.*

"I've been assigned in-house work. That means they either don't trust me or think I'm doing some bad stuff. Will keep you posted on any news.

"By the way, the bird is fine. Love, N."

"Okay, so translate," Janie said.

"She doesn't know much about Charlie and the Shairtons," Mark said.

"What's the bird she was talking about?"

"Phoenix. He's okay."

"Think we ought to head back that way?" Vicki said.

Mark shook his head. "Not until there's a good reason."

Judd took a deep breath as Leon Fortunato and a group of followers approached Z-Van's wheelchair. Judd adjusted his robe and pulled his turban as low as it would go.

"I'm so glad to hear that the report of your death was a little—premature!" Fortunato said, laughing at his own joke.

"I was just writing a new song about the potentate," Z-Van said.

"How wonderful. Music can help the grieving process. Would you be willing to perform it for us tomorrow?"

"At the funeral?"

"Of course. You could sing it when we introduce the potentate from the United North American States."

"I have to finish it first, but okay."

"Good. Oh, I want you to meet another artist who is putting the finishing touches on the statue we'll unveil tomorrow."

A man in colorful clothes daintily

stretched out a hand and greeted Z-Van. "I'm Guy Blod. I've been a great admirer of yours for years. You have my sympathy about your injury."

"I'd rather be in a wheelchair than in the ground," Z-Van said. He looked at Fortunato. "Any truth to the rumor that you'll be the next potentate?"

Fortunato smiled. "We are moving one step at a time and trying not to get ahead of ourselves."

"Yeah, you're probably on the trail of the assassin."

"Interesting you should say that. After careful review of the video, we have discovered the potentate's last words were an expression of forgiveness to the person who committed this heinous crime. The doctor who performed the autopsy said there was no human explanation for the potentate's ability to speak at all, given the extent of the damage done by the bullet."

Judd flinched, then raised a hand to adjust his turban.

"You mean he shouldn't have been able to talk," Z-Van said.

"Yes. Forgiveness such as this is surely divine." Fortunato looked up at the casket and the people passing by. "This was a good and righteous man. Truly, he was the son of god."

"Which is why we have erected such a statue to proclaim his divinity," Guy Blod said.

"As a matter of fact," Fortunato continued, "many believe there's a place for worshiping and even praying to our fallen leader."

Judd's mouth dropped and he stared at Fortunato. The man squinted at Judd. "This young man looks familiar."

"These are the guys who pulled the boss out of the rubble in Jerusalem," Westin said.

"Worshiping Carpathia," Z-Van said, "not a bad idea. I'll include it in the song."

"Wonderful," Fortunato said, unable to take his eyes off Judd. "If you will excuse us, we need to greet the people. Please call my assistant later about the details of the ceremony."

Fortunato and his lackeys moved to the middle of the line snaking toward the glass coffin. People bowed and knelt and kissed his hands.

"I can't take any more of this," Judd whispered to Lionel.

Westin pointed to the many concession stands and tents scattered about the plaza. "I heard on the news that it's supposed to get above one hundred degrees tomorrow."

Judd saw some emergency medical tents scattered around, but with a crowd expected nearly twice the size of the one at the Jerusalem Gala, he wondered how people would make it in the sweltering heat.

As they rode to the hotel in a special GC vehicle, Judd noticed people with sleeping bags on the sidewalk. Others had built lean-tos with cardboard boxes or slept in parks or hotel lobbies.

"You two will stay with us in the penthouse suite," Z-Van said.

"Have you decided when we'll head to the States?" Lionel said.

"I'll let you know."

Their hotel was jammed with people. Many were sharing rooms with other families. Judd and Lionel helped Z-Van to their room while Westin ran errands. The room was cool compared with the evening heat of New Babylon. Z-Van wheeled to his side of the suite and turned up the stereo to an earsplitting level.

Judd and Lionel retreated to the other side and changed out of their robes. They found two king-size beds and crawled in.

"I feel guilty for sleeping in this kind of luxury while other people are on the street," Lionel said.

Judd nodded. "Do you think it's happened yet?"

"You mean Carpathia? No. And Leon acted like he didn't have a clue about what's going to happen."

"Maybe Tsion's wrong."

Lionel sighed. "That would be a first."

"Do you realize we spent the day with one of the most famous musicians on the planet and stood next to the most famous political figure alive?"

Lionel chuckled. "And I couldn't wait for old Leon to leave. I thought he was going to recognize you."

"I'm just glad he didn't ask me what I thought about praying to Carpathia. Made me want to throw up."

"What's our plan for tomorrow?"

Judd closed his eyes and thought of the rest of the Young Tribulation Force. "We do whatever it takes to get back home."

TEN

Z-Van's Song

LIONEL awoke early on Sunday morning and checked e-mail. A message from Sam explained the details of the reports he had seen from Jerusalem.

> It was incredible to watch. The witnesses were bold, even with the GC there. Mr. Stein was among them, preaching, teaching, and pleading with the people to ask God's forgiveness.
>
> Mr. Stein believes we are seeing the fulfillment of prophecies that speak of many coming to Messiah before the end. I had second thoughts about going with you, but this confirms I made a good decision. I will be the Young Tribulation Force contact in Jerusalem.

Sam wrote that he was praying for Lionel and Judd each day and would also pray for their friends in the States.

Someone knocked at the door. Lionel opened it to find a man with long curly hair, tight jeans, and an open-collared shirt. He carried a guitar case. "Z-Van here?" the man mumbled.

"Yeah, come in."

The man stumbled inside and dropped the guitar. "Where is he?"

Lionel pointed to Z-Van's room, and the man walked in without knocking.

"Boomer!" Z-Van yelled. "Get your stick. Gotta teach you a new song."

Lionel took a walk outside the hotel. The streets were already crowded with people heading toward the plaza. They trudged by, some weeping, others staring off. Lionel knew they were worried about their future without Carpathia. They should worry about what they're going to do when he comes back, Lionel thought.

The temperature was already in the high eighties, and Lionel wondered how hot it would be by noon. Street vendors set up stands as people moved closer to the funeral site. Dealers sold umbrellas, bottled water, chairs, sunscreen, and even souvenirs. Every block featured street entertainers—some with guitars, others with different musical instruments. The farther away from the hotel Lionel walked, the rowdier the entertainment became. Jugglers and clowns tried to make people laugh who didn't want to laugh. Fortune-tellers badgered the grieving pilgrims to spend a few Nicks.

A fight broke out between a man playing a saxophone and one of the clowns. Peacekeepers quickly converged and broke it up. Lionel had seen enough. He went back to find Judd.

Vicki relieved Mark at the computer. He had answered questions and posted information on the Web site all day, and Vicki knew he had to be exhausted. "We'll wake you when the funeral begins or if something happens with Carpathia."

The house was quiet except for the droning of the television. She found no new information on Tsion Ben-Judah's Web site, so she clicked on the kids' Web site to retrieve e-mail. Kids from around the world were still writing and a few were angry.

I hope you and that Tsion Ben-Judah die! one person wrote. *You're probably glad Potentate*

Carpathia was killed. Well, one day it's going to happen to you and I hope I'm there to see it.

Another person wrote specifically to Vicki. You cheated us out of a great concert with The Four Horsemen. I hope the Global Community hunts you down like a dog and makes you pay for what you did, you religious freak!

Most of the e-mails asked specific questions about the future and how to become a true believer in Jesus. The computer blipped and a message from Natalie popped up.

> I'm at a safe computer. The farmhouse was destroyed, but the Shairtons and Charlie got out. They're in GC custody and seem to be okay. But the GC is asking questions about the adult Tribulation Force hideout. I don't know why.
>
> With what happened in Jerusalem Friday and the crackdown that's sure to come against believers, I don't think it's a good idea to leave them in the GC's hands. I have an idea on how to get them out, but I need some help. Can you suggest anyone?

Vicki hit the reply button and typed quickly. She gave Natalie information about two of their friends, Zeke Jr. and Lenore Barker.

We'll come back and help, Vicki wrote. We'll

*do anything to help get them out. Also, I used a
phone that belonged to Maxwell Stahley, one of
the GC's higher-ups. Can you check and make
sure that phone isn't being traced? If it is, we
have to get out of here.*

Vicki sent the message and responded to
a few more e-mails. The GC CNN coverage
showed live shots of people filing past
Nicolae Carpathia's body. Huge screens
had been placed throughout the massive
plaza and as far as a mile away. Estimates
were that as many as four million people
would jam the plaza to witness the farewell
to Carpathia.

Vicki shook her head. *When is it going to
happen?*

Judd and Lionel rode with Z-Van, Boomer,
and Westin to the back of the stage. Z-Van
invited them to stay while he performed, but
Judd said they wanted to join the crowd and
meet later at the hotel.

Judd looked out on a sea of people—every
nationality, color, ethnic background, and
religion were represented. People packed
together at the front trying to get a glimpse of
the stage and the world leaders. A canopy
sheltered Carpathia's coffin and the dignitaries

from the relentless sun, but people in the crowd fainted and had to be rushed to medical tents.

Judd and Lionel pushed through the crowd. Without a cloud in the sky, the heat was suffocating. Judd was glad he had the turban to cover his head, but any exposed skin burned quickly. Lionel touched Judd's shoulder and pointed to a temperature gauge on a huge television screen. It read 106 degrees.

"Why did you want to come out here?" Lionel said. "We could have stayed backstage out of the sun."

"In a crowd this size there have to be a few other believers."

Throughout the vast courtyard were numbered markers, each staffed by a Global Community Peacekeeper. They were about a half mile away from the stage when Judd stopped. Near marker 53 he spotted a female Peacekeeper talking with a GC official. Both had the marks of the believer.

Judd pointed them out to Lionel, and they pushed their way through the crowd. By the time they reached the Peacekeeper, the GC official was gone.

"Can I help you?" the Peacekeeper said as Judd and Lionel drew closer.

Judd tipped his turban, revealing the mark on his forehead. The Peacekeeper's mouth dropped open. "If you need some assistance, come right this way."

The woman took them to her station under a small canopy and gave them both a bottle of cold water from a cooler. Judd introduced himself and Lionel and told the Peacekeeper where they were from.

"I'm Annie Christopher," the woman said. She had short, dark hair and dark eyes.

"Who was that guy that was just here?" Lionel said.

Annie smiled. "My boss. He pulled me into his office one day after I'd prayed and told me I had a mark. We've been working together ever since."

Judd pointed to the draped statue behind Carpathia's body. "Do you know what they're going to do with that thing?"

Annie's radio crackled and she held up a hand. "Sector 53 contained," she said. She put the radio back and sighed. "My boss took a close look at it this morning. They have a fire going inside the statue that was started using Bibles and other holy books. Evidently they got them from the late Pontifex Maximus's collection.

"And that's not all. They want the statue to appear alive so they've somehow made the thing talk."

"You've got to be kidding," Judd said.

Annie shook her head. "On the scaffold this morning, my boss swears he heard the thing say in Carpathia's voice, 'I shall shed the blood of saints and prophets.' "

Judd shuddered and wondered what kind of recording device would work inside a burning statue. "Is that really Carpathia in that glass coffin?"

"As far as we can tell."

A bullhorn from the stage quieted the crowd. Judd watched the shimmering waves of heat rise from the pavement.

"Maybe we can talk later," Annie said.

"Thanks for your time," Judd said as they moved back into the sun. A glance at one of the huge screens showed that the ten regional potentates and other GC dignitaries were in place. Orchestra members arrived, and an announcer's voice boomed over the public-address system.

"Ladies and gentlemen, Global Community Supreme Commander Leon Fortunato and the administration of the one-world government would like to express sincere thanks and appreciation for your presence at the memorial service for former Supreme Potentate Nicolae J. Carpathia. Please honor the occasion by removing head coverings during the performance by the Global

Community International Orchestra of the anthem, 'Hail, Carpathia, Loving, Divine, and Strong.' "

Singers and a troupe of interpretive dancers joined the orchestra. After the performance, a montage of Carpathia's life was shown on the huge screens. Scenes included Nicolae at his fifth birthday party in Romania, his high school graduation, taking office as president of Romania, and speaking at the United Nations three and a half years before.

Fighter jets screamed overhead as video clips showed Carpathia mocking and challenging Eli and Moishe at the Wailing Wall. The ocean of viewers roared as Carpathia shot them dead.

"You notice they didn't show Eli and Moishe rising," Lionel said.

"That's just a silly myth," Judd smirked.

The montage switched to the closing night of the Gala and the slow-motion replay of Nicolae's demise. The body was loaded onto a GC helicopter. As it rose, the chopper was enveloped into a larger image of a man in a dark suit, standing among the stars, looking down on the crowd. It was Nicolae Carpathia.

The jets flew past as the crowd roared its approval. They understood the message:

Nicolae may be dead, but because he is divine, he still lives in the hearts of the faithful.

Judd turned to Lionel. "Next up on the program is a group of children singing 'Nicolae loves me, this I know.' "

The music faded and Leon Fortunato gave Carpathia's personal history in a voice filled with emotion. Nicolae had been born thirty-six years earlier in Roman, Romania, and was an only child. He was athletic and interested in academics. Before the age of twelve he was elected president of the Young Humanists and was valedictorian in high school and at the university he attended.

Fortunato recounted the story of Carpathia speaking at the United Nations after the global vanishings and said the world needed "someone to take us by the hand and lead us through the minefields of our own making and into the blessedness of hope.

"How could we have known that our prayers would be answered by one who would prove his own divinity over and over as he humbly, selflessly served, giving of himself even to the point of death to show us the way to healing?"

The crowd applauded. Judd glanced at Annie Christopher and saw her looking through binoculars.

Leon introduced the regional potentates.

When they were called, music from the region and loud cheering from his people greeted each potentate. When one potentate mentioned religion in his remarks, Fortunato stood and blasted Jews and followers of Tsion Ben- Judah. He blamed the Judah-ites for Carpathia's assassination and called them closed-minded for believing there was only one way to God.

Suddenly, the statue to Leon's left billowed black smoke. Leon turned and said jokingly, "Even Nicolae the Great has to agree with that."

Fortunato raised a hand as the crowd reacted. "But seriously, before our next potentate comes, let me reiterate. Any cult, sect, religion, or individual who professes a single avenue to God or heaven or bliss in the afterlife is the greatest danger to the global community. Such a view causes division, hatred, bigotry, and pride."

Fortunato then introduced the potentate of the United North American States. "But before he comes, we have a special treat for you. Here with music from the region and a new song written especially for this day is the lead singer for The Four Horsemen, Z-Van!"

The crowd cheered as Z-Van was wheeled onto the stage. Some who had not heard that

he was alive covered their mouths and cried.
Boomer plugged in an acoustic guitar and sat
on a stool a few feet away.

   Z-Van started the song a cappella; then
Boomer joined him.

> One man, one heart, one world,
>   one soul
> United with a common goal.
> To see the flag of peace held high
> We honor this man, Nicolae.
>
> One spinning bullet can't stop his song
> That rang in our hearts for so long.
> Beneath the rubble of our lives
> No force can silence Nicolae.

   As Boomer strummed, Z-Van moved in his
wheelchair. He seemed to want to get up and
run toward the crowd, but he couldn't. He
spoke/screamed the words:

> This man lies in state before you,
> Sealed in a man-made coffin.
> But no man can seal his ideas or his love.
> No force on earth can kill what he stood
>   for,
> What he strived for,
> The peace he fought for,
> And the dream he died for.

*Worship him now with your heart and soul.
Worship Nicolae!*

The crowd went wild and clapped along as
the orchestra joined in the simple tune.
When Z-Van had finished, millions stood
and cheered. There seemed no end to the
hype, but Judd wondered if something worse
was ahead. Would Nicolae rise from the dead
in front of the cameras beaming the ceremony to every spot on the planet?

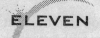

ELEVEN

Death on the Platform

JUDD felt the effects of the sweltering heat. With the sun beating down from a cloudless sky, he wondered how anyone could stand the soaring temperatures. As the next potentate stood to speak, Judd found a vendor selling lukewarm bottles of water. He bought two and returned to Lionel.

"This guy's speech is falling flat," Lionel said. "There's no emotion."

The potentate, Enoch Litwala, concluded his speech by saying, "The United African States opposes violence and deplores this senseless act by a misguided individual, ignorantly believing what has been spoon-fed him and millions of others who refuse to think for themselves."

Litwala sat and Fortunato seemed caught off

guard. He introduced the next two potentates, who also spoke without much emotion.

"I guess there are at least three regions that don't follow Carpathia too closely," Lionel said.

The crowd grew restless and many stood, wanting their chance to pass by the coffin. Fortunato calmed them and asked for attention to his final remarks.

"It should be clear to even the most casual observer that this is more than a funeral for a great leader, that the man who lies before you transcends human existence. Yes, yes, you may applaud. Who could argue such sentiments? I am pleased to report that the image you see to my left, your right, though larger than life, is an exact replica of Nicolae Carpathia, worthy of your reverence, yea, worthy of your worship.

"Should you feel inclined to bow to the image after paying your respects, feel free. Bow, pray, sing, gesture—do whatever you wish to express your heart. And believe. Believe, people, that Nicolae Carpathia is indeed here in spirit and accepts your praise and worship. Many of you know that this so-called man, whom I know to be divine, personally raised me from the dead."

"We've heard it just about every time he opens his mouth," Lionel whispered.

Judd chuckled, then quickly focused on Fortunato. The crowd no longer seemed antsy.

"I am no director, but let me ask the main television camera to move in on my face. Those close enough can look into my eyes. Those remote may look into my eyes on the screen."

"Don't look at him," Judd whispered.

Fortunato lowered his voice and spoke slowly. "Today I am instituting a new, improved global faith that shall have as its object of worship this image, which represents the very spirit of Nicolae Carpathia. Listen carefully, my people. When I said a moment ago that you may worship this image and Nicolae himself if you felt so inclined, I was merely being polite. Silence, please."

Four million people fell deathly silent. Fortunato told the crowd that they had a responsibility to submit to the authorities.

"As your new ruler, it is only fair of me to tell you that there is no option as it pertains to worshiping the image and spirit of Nicolae Carpathia. He is not only part of our new religion, but he is also its centerpiece. Indeed, he has become and forever shall *be* our religion. Now, before you bow before the image, let me impress upon your mind the consequences of disobeying such an order."

Rumbling shook the plaza. Fortunato

backed slightly away from the podium and looked toward the statue. A huge plume of black smoke billowed forth and blotted out the sun. A voice thundered from the statue, "I am the lord your god who sits high above the heavens!"

The crowd fell on their faces, terrified. Judd thought the voice sounded just like Carpathia. Judd and Lionel sat on the hot ground, not wanting to block anyone's view but not willing to kneel. Judd had made up his mind long ago that he would never worship any leader but God.

"I am the god above all other gods. There is none like me. Worship or beware!"

Fortunato leaned over the microphone and spoke gently, like a concerned father to little children. "Fear not. Lift your eyes to the heavens." Leon paused as the smoky cloud disappeared. "Nicolae Carpathia loves you and has only your best in mind. Charged with the responsibility of ensuring compliance with the worship of your god, I have also been imbued with power. Please stand."

As people stood, Lionel turned to Judd. "What kind of power?"

Judd shrugged as Fortunato turned and looked at the ten potentates. Three of them glared at Leon.

"Let us assume that there may be those here

who choose, for one reason or another, to refuse to worship Carpathia. Perhaps they are independent spirits. Perhaps they are rebellious Jews. Perhaps they are secret Judah-ites who still believe 'their man' is the only way to God. Regardless of their justification, they shall surely die."

People gasped and stepped back.

"Marvel not that I say unto you that some shall surely die. If Carpathia is not god and I am not his chosen one, then I shall be proved wrong. If Carpathia is not *the* only way and *the* only life, then what I say is not *the* only truth and none should fear."

Vicki and the others gathered as the service in New Babylon started. It was early in the morning in Wisconsin, but no one complained. Some of the kids thought that Tsion might be wrong. Maybe Carpathia wasn't the Antichrist. Perhaps, they said, Leon Fortunato was. When Leon started his hypnotic speech, Vicki leaned close. The camera stayed on Leon's face, and Vicki wondered if people watching around the world would be affected like those in New Babylon.

"It is also only fair that I offer proof of my role," Fortunato said, "in addition to what you have already seen and heard from Nicolae Carpathia's own image. I call on the power of my most high god to prove that he rules from heaven by burning to death with his pure fire those who would oppose me, those who would deny his deity, those who would subvert and plot and scheme to take my rightful place as his spokesman!" Leon paused dramatically. Then, "I pray he does this even as I speak!"

He pointed at three potentates sitting at the end of the platform. Vicki shielded her eyes from the screen as white-hot flames burst from the sky and torched the three. The seven other potentates jumped out of their seats and backed away to avoid the heat and flames.

"I've never seen Carpathia do anything like that," Janie said. "Maybe this Fortunato guy is the real Antichrist."

The kids stared in disbelief as the camera focused on Fortunato. The man smiled as he watched the three potentates burn.

People around Judd screamed and wailed but stayed in their places, paralyzed with fear. As quickly as the fire shot from the sky and burned the three potentates, it disappeared, leaving three tiny piles of ash.

Fortunato assured those who lived in the

three potentates' regions that replacement potentates had already been selected.

Judd turned to Lionel. "I wonder what else they've already planned?"

Lionel glanced at Global Community Peacekeepers and guards placed around the plaza. "What'll we do if they make everybody bow to the statue?"

Judd gulped a drink of warm water and pursed his lips. "It's going to be hard to enforce a rule on four million people."

Fortunato encouraged the frightened crowd to express their approval. "You need not fear your lord god. What you have witnessed here shall never befall you if you love Nicolae with the love that brought you here to honor his memory. Now before the interment, once everyone has had a chance to pay last respects, I invite you to come and worship. Come and worship. Worship your god, your dead yet living king."

People nearby fell to their knees and wept. Some lifted hands and seemed to be praying to Carpathia. Officials removed the barricade in front of the viewing line, and slowly people began to walk past Carpathia's coffin. The seven remaining potentates shook hands with Fortunato, leaning close to him to say a few words.

"What do you think they're saying?" Judd said.

"Nice shot?"

In an act Judd couldn't believe was shown on camera, Fortunato stepped to the empty chairs and swept the ashes of the dead potentates away. When the chairs were clean, he clapped and rubbed his hands together and let the dust fall away.

Judd turned to the thermometer fastened to the side of a medical tent. It read 109 degrees. He looked for Annie Christopher, but she wasn't under the GC canopy.

"Look at this," Lionel said.

The statue began to sway and bounce, as if another earthquake was on its way, but no other structures moved. People whispered and pointed as word spread through the crowd. The rocking and swaying continued as the image turned red. Smoke belched and formed black clouds that hovered over the assembly. With the sun blocked, the temperature fell. Many lay with their faces on the ground, terrified.

"Get out of here now," someone whispered to Judd. It was Annie. "This place isn't safe for believers."

"Where should we go?" Judd said.

"Anywhere but here. Just don't make it obvious. Don't run."

At the edges of the crowd people screamed and ran wildly. Annie broke away and headed for a cart. "Stop!" she screamed at the frightened people. "Stay where you are and you won't be hurt!"

The statue roared, "Fear not and flee not! Flee not or you shall surely die!"

A blinding flash knocked Judd and Lionel to the ground. Seconds later thunder shook the earth. Many of those who ran had been struck by lightning from the hovering cloud.

Judd noticed a crowd standing around the nearby cart and pushed his way through. A uniformed GC officer lay on the ground, her head scorched by a lightning bolt. It was Annie. She had been killed instantly.

"Back away!" a guard said to the group.

Judd and Lionel walked a few paces. The statue continued its angry howling. "You would defy *me*? Be silent! Be still! Fear not! Flee not! And behold!"

Above them, the smoky clouds rolled and churned until the black mixed with red and purple. Like a prelude to some demonic performance, the clouds signaled what was about to come. Judd thought he had seen ultimate evil when he had

witnessed the horsemen and the sting-
ing locusts, but this was even more terrify-
ing.

The statue shook and said, "Gaze not
upon me." Smoke stopped and the statue
was still. It said, "Gaze upon your lord
god."

All eyes turned to the coffin where Carpathia lay, and the camera zoomed in on his
face. The screen was split—with one side
staying on the dead man's face, the other side
showing his entire body.

In only a few minutes the temperature had
fallen from 109 to the low sixties, and people
shivered and rubbed their arms. Lights shone
on the coffin.

Judd studied one of the monitors. He
thought he saw movement.

"Did you see that?" Lionel said.

"His hand?"

"Yeah. Creepy."

"There it goes again," Judd said. Carpathia
lifted a finger, then let it fall. He uncurled his
left index finger and it looked like it was
pointing.

Lightning struck the stage and Carpathia's
hands moved to his sides. Judd looked
closely and saw the man's chest rising and
falling. Carpathia was breathing.

Vicki couldn't take her eyes off the coverage. The news anchor was speechless as Carpathia's hand moved. Cameras showed anxious faces twisted in terror in the crowd. As the camera panned the stage, several surviving potentates fell to their knees.

The screen split into four camera shots. One quadrant showed Fortunato and the potentates, two others focused on the crowd, and the upper left corner stayed on Carpathia's face. Suddenly, Nicolae's eyes popped open. Several kids in the room screamed.

"Take a look at neon Leon," Conrad said. "He just turned white as a sheet and can't stop shaking."

"He thought he was going to be the next potentate," Vicki said. "Not anymore."

Nicolae's lips separated, and he lifted his head slightly until it touched the transparent lid. The crowd at the front of the platform and all the dignitaries collapsed. Carpathia lifted his knees and kicked something with his left leg.

"He just broke the vacuum seal," Conrad said. "He's going to try and get out of there, but the glass alone has to weigh a hundred pounds."

The once-dead potentate brought his hands and knees up and pushed at the lid, ripping bolts from the Plexiglas. He kept pushing until the glass popped open and crashed into the podium, knocking it over.

Since everyone else was on the ground, Judd and Lionel sat, as people shrieked and moaned across the plaza.

"What now?" Lionel said.

Judd couldn't take his eyes off Carpathia. "Let's stay here until we figure out what to do."

Carpathia sprang from the coffin like a cat and stood in the narrow end, facing the crowd. Instead of cheering, the stunned crowd was silent.

"Don't they sew your lips together when you're dead?" Lionel said.

"I don't know," Judd said. He remembered the triumph and glee he felt when Eli and Moishe had risen into the sky. Now he felt the exact opposite as he watched Nicolae Carpathia standing in his own coffin.

Nicolae looked like he had just stepped off the pages of a men's fashion magazine. His shoes gleamed, his suit pristine, every hair in place. Judd held his breath as Nicolae raised his hands and began to speak.

TWELVE

Dead Man Talking

WHEN Carpathia moved, Vicki backed away from the television. As he stood before millions in New Babylon and countless numbers of viewers, a chill ran up her spine. Tsion had been right. Carpathia was now inhabited by Satan himself.

Behind Nicolae, Fortunato and the seven potentates were on their knees, crying and wailing openly. The microphone had been knocked over by the coffin lid, but Nicolae's voice was crystal clear on the television.

"Peace," Carpathia said. "Be still." The camera kept a close-up on Nicolae's face, and Vicki noticed the scene seemed to get brighter. The dark smoke that had hung over the gathering vanished, and the sun came back.

"Peace be unto you," he said. "My peace I give you. Please stand."

As people throughout the plaza rose, Mark

hurried to the computer. "We have to make sure kids know what's going on."

Carpathia continued. "Let not your hearts be troubled. Believe in me."

Conrad shook his head. "This guy is as counterfeit as they come. Those are Jesus' words."

With his hands still raised, Carpathia said, "You marvel that I speak directly to your hearts without amplification, yet you saw me raise myself from the dead. Who but the most high god has power over death? Who but god controls the earth and sky?"

"Vicki, come here!" Mark said.

Carpathia's voice was gentle and soothing. "Do you still tremble? Are you still sore afraid? Fear not, for I bring you good tidings of great joy. It is I who loves you who stands before you today, wounded unto death but now living . . . for you. For you.

"You need never fear me, for you are my friends. Only my enemies need fear. Why are you fearful, O you of little faith? Come to me, and you will find rest for your souls."

Carpathia's speaking more words of Jesus sickened Vicki. She moved to Mark's side and looked at the computer where Mark had pulled up a new message from Natalie: *Cell call traced to Wisconsin. Get out now.*

Judd and Lionel stood with four million others as the sun warmed the plaza again. Within minutes, the temperature had climbed back over one hundred. People were in shock about Carpathia, and only his comforting voice had calmed them enough to obey.

"Only he who is not with me is against me," Carpathia continued. "Anyone who speaks a word against me, it will not be forgiven him. But as for you, the faithful, be of good cheer. It is I; do not be afraid."

Judd glanced back and saw two guards loading Annie's body onto one of the carts. Judd wondered if they were setting up a morgue for all who had been struck by lightning.

"I want to greet you," Carpathia said. "Come to me, touch me, talk to me, worship me. All authority has been given to me in heaven and on earth. I will be with you always, even to the end."

People standing in line remained frozen, too frightened to move. Carpathia turned and nodded to someone. "Urge my own to come to me." Slowly, people approached the stairs. "And as you come, let me speak to you about my enemies. . . ."

"Uh-oh," Lionel whispered. "Maybe it's time to get out of here."

Judd shook his head. "Why don't you go back to the hotel. I'll stay."

"What if he makes everyone kneel before him and call him lord?"

"Shh!" a woman next to Judd said.

"I have to stay and see this," Judd whispered. "Go back to the hotel and wait. We'll try to get out of here tonight."

As Lionel slowly slipped into the crowd, Carpathia continued, still standing in his coffin. "You all know me as a forgiving potentate. Ironically, the person or persons responsible for my demise may no longer be pursued for murder. Attempted murder of a government official is still an international felony, of course. The guilty know who they are, but as for me, I hereby pardon any and all. No official action is to be taken by the government of the Global Community. What steps fellow citizens may take to ensure that such an act never takes place again, I do not know and will not interfere with.

"However, individual would-be assassins aside, there are opponents to the Global Community and to my leadership. Hear me, my people: I need not and will not tolerate opposition. You need not fear because you came here to commemorate my life on the occasion of my death, and you remain to worship me as your divine leader. But to those who believe it is possible to rebel against my authority and survive, beware. I shall soon institute a program of loyalty confirmation that will prove once and for all who is with us and who is against us, and woe to the haughty insurrectionist. He will find no place to hide.

"Now, loyal subjects, come and worship."

Loyalty confirmation, Judd thought. *That doesn't sound good.*

Lionel crouched low as he moved through the crowd, trying not to block anyone's view. He noticed a GC guard a few yards ahead and angled away from him. The guard spotted Lionel and yelled, "Halt!"

Lionel stopped and looked around, pretending he didn't know who the guard was talking to.

"Where are you going?"

"Back to my hotel. I don't feel well."

"Your potentate has just risen from the dead. You will stay and listen." The guard squinted at him. "Unless you are an enemy of the Global Community."

Lionel swooned, as if he were about to

faint. "I thought I'd watch the televised coverage. . . ." He fell to one knee, and the guard helped him to his feet.

The guard pointed. "There's a medical assistance tent there."

"Thank you," Lionel said. He limped toward the tent, went to the other side, and kept moving through the crowd.

Vicki and the others hastily gathered their things, listening to the audio from New Babylon. Not long after Nicolae began speaking, the GC CNN logo featured the words *Day of Resurrection*.

Vicki knew they couldn't dawdle. If Natalie was right, the GC could find them any moment.

"You'd think the GC would let their people take a day off for the funeral," Darrion said.

"It's not a funeral anymore," Mark said, "and I don't care what Nicolae says about forgiveness, we have to stay one step ahead of these people."

They all loaded their things into the back of the Suburban. Shelly took a long look at the Stahley summer home. "It would have been a great hideout."

"Turn on the radio so we can hear what's going on," Janie said.

Mark turned the key and nothing happened. He tried everything but the car wouldn't start.

Judd watched the screen carefully as people passed Carpathia, some shaking hands, others fainting before they even reached him.

Carts with bullhorns zigzagged through the crowd telling everyone that "only those already inside the courtyard will be able to greet His Excellency personally. Thanks for understanding, and do feel free to remain for final remarks in an hour or so."

Lionel found the hotel nearly empty, a few desk workers gathered around a television. He ran to the elevator and went to Z-Van's suite, but his heart dropped when he realized he didn't have a key. The door was locked.

Lionel knocked on the door and waited. Nothing. *If I ask for a key they'll think I'm a crazy fan.*

Lionel moved to the elevator and stepped inside just as the door to the suite opened.

He rushed back into the suite and found Westin, Z-Van's pilot, wide-eyed and jittery.

"I was backstage when Carpathia moved. Z-Van just stared at the guy and didn't move. I said, 'Don't you remember what that kid told you?' But Z-Van wouldn't listen. I came back here alone."

"I came to get our stuff," Lionel said. "We're going to try and get out tonight."

"No! Not before you tell me what I have to do."

"What do you mean?" Lionel said.

"You guys were right. Carpathia came back to life just like you said. And if you're right about that, you must be right about Jesus. Tell me what I have to do to become one of you."

Lionel turned down the sound on the TV and grabbed a Bible. "This is how we know what's true. The prophecies about Carpathia and what's going on in the world are all in here."

"I believe you," Westin said. "Hurry before he calls down lightning on us all."

Lionel showed Westin the passage in the book of John where a man named Nicodemus came to Jesus and asked what he had to do to be saved. "Jesus said you have to be born again."

"I've heard that before," Westin said.

"It means you have to ask God to come into your life. You can't save yourself because you're a sinner and sin separates you from God." Lionel showed him a verse in Romans that said everyone has sinned. "Nobody else but God can help you."

"I believe that, so what do I do?"

Lionel pointed to John 3:16 and Westin read it aloud. " 'For God so loved the world that he gave his only Son, so that everyone who believes in him will not perish but have eternal life.' " Westin closed the Bible and said, "I want that."

"Then pray with me," Lionel said. As Lionel spoke, Westin repeated his words aloud. "Dear God, I need you right now. I believe that you're the only one who can save me from my sin. I believe Jesus paid for the bad things I've done by dying on the cross. He is the true Son of God who was raised from the dead. I ask you to forgive me and save me. I want you to be the leader of my life right now. You are the true king, the real Potentate, and I want to follow you from this day forward. In Jesus' name, amen."

Lionel looked at Westin and saw the mark of the true believer, a cross, on the pilot's forehead. Lionel explained what the sign meant, and Westin said he wanted to hear more.

Lionel smiled. Helping someone come to know God gave him an indescribable feeling. Every time people asked God to forgive them, they went from death to life, from Carpathia's kingdom to the kingdom of God.

Lionel glanced at the television as Nicolae Carpathia moved toward one of the cameras. "Let's watch what the enemy's up to."

Vicki and the others took their things and bolted from the Suburban. Darrion showed them a hiding place in the rocks high above the Stahley home. Mark, Conrad, Shelly, and Janie pushed the car down the driveway and onto the road. Mark tried to start it again, but the battery was dead. They pushed it into some brush, hoping the GC wouldn't find it if they did come, but not wanting to take any chances.

When they were together above the house, Mark opened the laptop and turned it on. "I want to see what Carpathia says."

Vicki put a hand on his arm and reached to turn the laptop off. Cars rumbled in the distance.

Lionel turned up the volume as an announcer said, "Ladies and gentlemen of the Global Community, your Supreme Potentate, His Excellency Nicolae Carpathia."

Carpathia smiled. "My dear subjects, we have, together, endured quite a week, have we not? I was deeply touched by the millions who made the effort to come to New Babylon for what turned out to be, gratefully, not my funeral. The outpouring of emotion was no less encouraging to me.

"As you know and as I have said, there remain small pockets of resistance to our cause of peace and harmony. There are even those who have made a career of saying the most hurtful, blasphemous, and false statements about me, using terms for me that no person would ever want to be called.

"I believe you will agree that I proved today who I am and who I am not. You will do well to follow your heads and your hearts and continue to follow me. You know what you saw, and your eyes do not lie."

"He's saying he's god," Lionel said. "He's going to convince a lot of people to follow him today."

"God's going to let him get away with it?" Westin said.

"Only for a while," Lionel said.

Carpathia invited anyone who was formerly against him to join the Global Community, then added, "In closing let me speak directly to the opposition. I have always allowed different points of view. There are those among you, however, who have referred overtly to me personally as the Antichrist and this period of history as the Tribulation. You may take the following as my personal pledge:

"If you insist on continuing with your subversive attacks on my character and on the world harmony I have worked so hard to create, the word *tribulation* will not begin to describe what is in store for you. If the last three and a half years are your idea of tribulation, wait until you endure the Great Tribulation."

ABOUT THE AUTHORS

Jerry B. Jenkins (www.jerryjenkins.com) is the writer of the Left Behind series. He owns the Jerry B. Jenkins Christian Writers Guild, an organization dedicated to mentoring aspiring authors. Former vice president for publishing for the Moody Bible Institute of Chicago, he also served many years as editor of *Moody* magazine and is now Moody's writer-at-large.

His writing has appeared in publications as varied as *Reader's Digest, Parade, Guideposts*, in-flight magazines, and dozens of other periodicals. Jenkins's biographies include books with Billy Graham, Hank Aaron, Bill Gaither, Luis Palau, Walter Payton, Orel Hershiser, and Nolan Ryan, among many others. His books appear regularly on the *New York Times, USA Today, Wall Street Journal,* and *Publishers Weekly* best-seller lists.

Jerry is also the writer of the nationally syndicated sports story comic strip *Gil Thorp,* distributed to newspapers across the United States by Tribune Media Services.

Jerry and his wife, Dianna, live in Colorado and have three grown sons.

Dr. Tim LaHaye (www.timlahaye.com), who conceived the idea of fictionalizing an account of the Rapture and the Tribulation, is a noted author, minister, and nationally recognized speaker on Bible prophecy. He is the founder of both Tim LaHaye Ministries and The PreTrib Research Center. He also recently cofounded the Tim LaHaye School of Prophecy at Liberty University. Presently Dr. LaHaye speaks at many of the major Bible prophecy conferences in the U.S. and Canada, where his current prophecy books are very popular.

Dr. LaHaye holds a doctor of ministry degree from Western Theological Seminary and a doctor of literature degree from Liberty University. For twenty-five years he pastored one of the nation's outstanding churches in San Diego, which grew to three locations. It was during that time that he founded two accredited Christian high schools, a Christian school system of ten schools, and Christian Heritage College.

Dr. LaHaye has written over forty books that have been published in more than thirty languages. He has written books on a wide variety of subjects, such as family life, temperaments, and Bible prophecy. His current fiction works, the Left Behind series, written with Jerry B. Jenkins, continue to appear on the bestseller lists of the Christian Booksellers Association, *Publishers Weekly*, *Wall Street Journal*, *USA Today*, and the *New York Times*.

He is the father of four grown children and grandfather of nine. Snow skiing, waterskiing, motorcycling, golfing, vacationing with family, and jogging are among his leisure activities.

The Future Is Clear

Check out the exciting Left Behind: The Kids series

BOOKS #27 AND #28 COMING SOON!

Hooked on the exciting
Left Behind: The Kids series?
Then you'll love the dramatic audios!

Listen as the characters come to life in this theatrical
audio that makes the saga of those left behind
even more exciting.

High-tech sound effects, original music,
and professional actors will have you
on the edge of your seat.

Experience the heart-stopping action and
suspense of the end times for yourself!

Three exciting volumes available on CD or cassette.